MANDRAKE AND A MURDER

THE WITCHES OF WORMWOOD MYSTERIES

RUBY LOREN

BOOKS IN THE SERIES

THE NEW WITCHES IN TOWN

Not many people move to Wormwood.

The South East of England is notorious for its expensive properties, but house prices in this town have stayed stagnant - much like the people who live here.

Unfortunately, I'm one of them.

My entire life had been geared towards getting away from Wormwood, but, like everyone else in town, I had my roots here. And those roots had a way of dragging you back to where you belonged... no matter how many years you stayed away.

Most of the towns and villages in the South East of England have a rich historical heritage. Many of these places have folklore that stretches back to tales of broomstick-flying witches and bets made with devils. But only one place still actively encourages belief in those old tales.

Wormwood has been trading off all things supernatural for over a century. The town has more psychics, fortunetellers, and witches for hire per capita than any other town in the country. Even Glastonbury doesn't come close to our level of woo-woo. All of that is a fact of life when you live here. You'll bump into a voodoo priest gathering gris gris in the graveyard, you'll witness the plague of black cats belonging to the town's witches running down the streets, or you'll happen upon druids picking mushrooms in the surrounding woods and fields. It's the kind of place where strange things go on every single day, and yet, somehow, nothing new ever happens. Like a pond with no water flowing in or out of it, Wormwood is a gloomy puddle of stagnation.

Or it was, before the murder.

I'm sure no one has ever said 'You know what this town needs? A violent murder to add some zest to daily affairs!' but that was the effect it had. No one could stop talking about the murder, and no one was safe from suspicion. After centuries of selling fake potions and charms to the dribs and drabs of tourists who ventured (often accidentally) through town, Wormwood was getting ready to tear itself apart.

It had happened yesterday morning.

Lara Rivers had been out walking her dog in the woods, away from the pack of marauding cats, when she'd come upon a terrible scene. Her walk had taken her to the clearing in the heart of Wormwood Forest where druids and witches liked to meet when the moon was full. I wouldn't have been surprised if her goal hadn't been a little bit of petty payback (in the form of dog fouling) for the witches' cats' violent attitude towards her canine companion, but what she'd discovered was far worse than an act of minor sabotage.

She'd found the body of a man, lying in the centre of the clearing with an ornate, bejewelled knife embedded in his chest. According to the local gossips, the corpse had been at the centre of some kind of magic ring, spray-painted onto the grass. There'd also been a proliferation of ominous symbols painted onto the trunks of the trees that surrounded the clearing in a circle. Depending on who you listened to, voodoo dolls, inverted crucifixes, silver coins, and all manner of other items each describer had associated with something really, really evil, had been present at the scene.

The police were baffled. No one seemed to know anything about the dead man apart from his name: Zack Baden, that had been written on the driver's licence he'd had in his pocket. And no one knew why he'd been killed in such a dramatic fashion.

It was the most exciting thing to happen in Wormwood since the witch trials, more than 400 years ago.

It was also the worst thing to ever happen to the town.

People liked to forget that Wormwood existed. It was amazing how many major roads had been built that inexplicably curved around the town at the last moment, and newcomers to the town were rarer than hen's teeth. But the murder could change all of that.

A lot of the visitors to my small apothecary were concerned about the spiritual implications of what had happened so close to the town. They feared demons were going to crawl up out of the earth and lay siege. I was more worried about consequences in the physical world. Growing up in Wormwood, there had always been weird, inexplicable things that just sort of happened. There were remarkable runs of luck, both good and bad, and people even occasionally just disappeared off the face of the earth. But this was an overt display of the worst things that were whispered about Wormwooders behind our backs.

It was going to be tough for anyone to forget about the town when it boasted a ritualistic unsolved murder. Some folks may even start wondering if there really was some kind of dark magic afoot in South East England.

"There's nothing like that going on here. No one's that evil. Even the ones who like to think they are," I said aloud, straightening some of the potted herbs I kept on the counter of the shop. I brushed strands of golden-brown hair back from my face where they had fallen loose from the French plait I'd unwisely attempted that morning, after YouTube had bolstered my confidence.

"If you're going to talk nonsense, the least you can do is offer me some coffee, so I can try to pretend to be interested," a voice replied.

"I was talking to myself. It's the only intelligent conversation I get around here. And no coffee! We've discussed this before." I narrowed my amber eyes, looking for the speaker.

A large black kitten - well on his way to becoming a proper cat - appeared from under the counter and stretched himself out, so he looked slim and sleek. I wished the same trick would work on me. "Hazel... The whole point of having a familiar is that you don't need to talk to yourself like a crazy person. I'm here to guide you, like cat Yoda. Cat Yoda who you should give coffee."

I looked down at the big kitten. He had a glazed look to his eyes that hinted he'd found his way into the catnip supply again. It was no wonder he now wanted a totally not cat-suitable caffeine fix. I would have to find a better hiding place. "But if I'm the only one who can understand you, isn't that almost the same as talking to myself? To anyone watching, I would look just as nuts." I considered. "Probably nuttier." Talking to a cat (and clearly pretending he was answering back) had to be worse than talking to yourself. "I'm still not convinced you really are talking to me."

"Are my lips moving?" Hemlock said, jumping up onto the counter and contorting his mouth into a wide pointy grin. He'd definitely been in the catnip.

"You don't really have lips."

"How dare you!" he said and began washing his bottom. No matter how many times I got carried away and credited

Hemlock with human-level intelligence, he would always remind me that he was a cat at heart by doing something that was utterly unacceptable in polite society.

I saw a slinking dark shape out of the corner of my eye as Hemlock's shadow, Hedge, trotted by. Hedge had turned up out of the blue at the same time as Hemlock. But whilst Hemlock had announced that he was my witch's familiar (and very nearly triggered a series of trips to a psychiatrist about the mental breakdown I had to be experiencing) Hedge had always remained silent. His quiet nature had been a big part of what had finally convinced me that I probably wasn't imagining the sarcastic kitten who'd started talking to me - and me alone. If I were really crazy, wouldn't I have imagined both of them yakking away?

I'd asked Hemlock where Hedge had come from, or what he was doing with him, but he'd said he didn't know. He also claimed that Hedge sometimes told him things, but I took that with a big pinch of salt. I didn't believe Hemlock could understand Hedge any better than I could. They'd arrived at the same time but whilst Hemlock felt compelled to stay as my familiar, there was no reason, beyond free food and lodging, that I could credit with the silent kitten's decision to hang around.

"Have you heard anything more about the murder?" I asked the black cat, once he'd finished washing, and I'd finished ignoring the horrible slurping noises he made whilst he did it.

"Nope. Everyone's gone silent. Too silent, if you ask me. I think the no-brains out there finally figured out that this might be bad for tourism. Not that this place is *Disney Land*..."

"Do you think it really will stop people coming here?" I was worrying about my little shop. I owned the lease and the property itself, but there were still certain costs I had to meet to make it worthwhile. Not to mention, I had to keep Hemlock and Hedge in cat food.

"Stop them... or bring them here. You should be careful. Matters like this can turn into a witch hunt. And in this town, it will be a literal one," Hemlock said, sounding smart and not at all sarcastic for a moment.

I shot him a surprised look. When he'd walked in and started talking to me for the very first time, I'd had the unfortunate duty of explaining to him that there had been some kind of a mistake. The terrible truth was, in a town filled to the brim of its pointy hat with witches, I was a dud.

I'd long believed that all 'magic' was merely a psychological tool used to imagine a goal into being... until Hemlock had happened. Then it had been pretty hard to ignore that there were some things psychology couldn't explain - especially when this particular *thing's* sole purpose in life seemed to be to judge me from the sidelines. Hemlock was not thrilled that he'd been assigned to a dud witch. He'd stuck around, but he loved to dish out disdain with a ladle. That was why I was surprised he seemed to be taking this murder so seriously.

"If there's a witch hunt, I should be just fine," I told him.

"Not necessarily."

A loud knocking sound from the front of the shop made me jump.

Hemlock jumped down from the counter and did his slinking run across the floor. "Changes are coming to this town..." he said, by way of an ominous farewell.

Is it the police? Are they here to arrest me? I thought, completely irrationally. Hemlock's talk of witch hunts and changes had put me on edge.

I knew I was innocent. I'd been tucked up in bed around the same time the murder must have been happening. But I was also painfully aware that the only person who could corroborate that alibi was furry and understood by me alone. As weird as Wormwood was, trying to claim that a cat could give you an alibi was pushing it.

When I looked out of the door of my still-closed shop, I discovered it wasn't the police calling. Not unless the police had recently changed their uniform from black kevlar vests and white shirts to pink feather boas and tartan scarves.

I unlocked the door and opened it up. Out of hours customers were an occasional occurrence. Usually, they happened at the tail end of the day when a witch or a magician was prepping for a night of spell-work and realised they'd run out of an essential ingredient. Morning visitors were something new - especially morning visitors who looked like they'd packed for a long trip.

"Hazel Salem?"

I nodded.

"Look at you! You're all grown up. We knew you would be... otherwise we wouldn't be here," the woman on the left said, talking as if she knew me. She was the one wearing the pink feather boa. It complemented the peroxide blonde Hollywood curls that clung to her head the way Marilyn Monroe's had. The bright pink lipstick was surely chosen to match the boa, and the rest of her outfit was equally ostentatious. It included an expensive looking cream coat and, most surprisingly of all, a pair of pink Doc Martins.

After all that, I'd expected stilettos.

"Can I help you?" I asked, smiling in what I hoped was a polite manner. I couldn't fight the feeling that there was something strange going on.

"Linda, she doesn't recognise us," the other woman said, looking at me over the top of her stylish glasses. Her hair was also blonde, but a far more mature and less 'look at me' champagne tone. She wore a sensible black trench coat and the only thing that jumped out at me was her bright green eyes and the tartan scarf she wore.

"I know she was just a baby, but I thought I made a really good impression!" the Marilyn-alike said.

"I'm sorry but... who are you?" I was fast getting the impression that this pair were not customers... and the suitcases they had with them were starting to alarm me.

The tartan-scarf wearer lifted a hand to her chest. "Allow me to introduce myself. I am your aunt, Minerva."

"And I'm Linda. Also your aunt," the other supplied.

"I didn't know I had aunts."

"That's just Freya all over, isn't it?" Linda rolled her eyes at Minerva. "She leaves her only child all of her problems to deal with but doesn't tell her about her family."

"Linda! We shouldn't speak ill of the dead. Your mother was a very interesting woman. She was wonderfully talented," Minerva said, addressing me. "We were very sorry to hear of her passing. I only wish we'd been able to come sooner, but we had some urgent business to attend to." Here she paused to give Linda a significant look. By the way Linda avoided making eye contact, I gathered that it was a silent instruction to keep quiet about whatever their 'business' had been. "The main thing is, we are here to help you now. How are your powers coming along?"

I did some rapid blinking. "Powers?"

The two women on the shop doorstep exchanged another glance.

"You do know you're a witch, don't you?" Linda ventured.

I started to nod and then turned it into a head wobble as I dithered. "I do. I mean... in the traditional sense of the word. My mother definitely believed she was a witch. A lot of people around here go in for that sort of thing."

Their expressions filled with horror.

"You haven't seen any signs of powers manifesting? How

old are you?" Minerva's forehead was creased with concern.

"I'm twenty-eight. And no... no powers. Unless you count Hemlock, my cat," I added, hoping that might be something to lift their obvious dismay.

"Leave me out of this," Hemlock muttered from some unseen vantage point.

"Stop spying on us!" I called out.

"What did you expect with a mother like Freya? She never told any of us who the father was. He could have been anyone! Perhaps he was so normal that his genes stamped all over ours. She doesn't even have the Salem green eyes," Linda said, looking ready to pull her hair out.

"Hang on a moment. Are you talking about your familiar?" Minerva looked hopeful.

"I think so. He says that only I can understand him. Is that correct?" I was still on the fence as to whether or not I really was nutty.

"She's got a familiar, Linda. She must have some magic in her. They only appear when things are about to change. How long have you had this cat?"

"He arrived when I moved back to Wormwood, about six months ago."

"When your mother passed away," Minerva observed.

I nodded. "She left the shop to me in her will. The will also said that her last wishes were for me to carry on the family business."

The will had put a spanner in the works of the life I'd planned out for myself - that and the colossal guilt I'd felt for not even realising my mother had been unwell. She'd hardly seemed to age at all when I'd been growing up. When I'd left home to pursue my writing career, she'd been supportive. We'd never been particularly close or shared many secrets together. Looking back, I supposed that was the reason why she hadn't called me back from my travels until it was too late. That, and I now suspected she'd wanted to guilt trip me into running the shop after she was gone.

It had worked.

"She had a good long life," Minerva said, smiling understandingly.

I nodded, knowing it would be impolite to correct her. My mother had been in her fifties, but had looked twenty years younger when I'd last seen her. It wasn't a particularly long life by any stretch, but I knew it was just one of the stock phrases people said when they wanted to express sympathy. It didn't mean anything.

We stood in silence for a moment, all three of us aware that the conversation had somehow veered sideways, and we didn't know how to pick it back up again.

"We're here to stay with you," Linda announced, lifting up a fussy-looking suitcase.

"Linda! We said we would take things slowly." Minerva turned back to face me. "We thought your mother might not have told you about us, but it is the family tradition that younger witches live with more mature witches, whilst they're developing their magic."

"I think I'm a little too old to get my *Hogwarts* letter," I told them.

"Contrary to popular culture, witches... real witches... come into their powers quite some time after their eleventh, or even sixteenth birthday. It's a good thing, too. Can you imagine what the world would be like if a bunch of teenagers were running around flinging spells in all directions? Some witches aren't even responsible when they're much, much older than a teenager." Minerva looked sideways at Linda when she said it.

Linda tutted and raised her gaze to the heavens. "Some witches are boring."

"You're here to stay with me?" I was really connecting the

dots quickly this morning.

"Yes. You've got plenty of space. We all used to live here when we were younger." Linda flicked a small strand of blonde hair off her made-up face.

My expression must have shown that I was faltering because Minerva tilted her head and smiled at me. "Don't worry for a second about not having magic yet. The most powerful witches of all time were late developers."

I opened my mouth to say that magic wasn't what I was worried about, but Linda got there first.

"Or you're just not magic at all. In which case... bad luck!"

"She has a familiar. They don't come out of the woodwork for non-witches."

"It could be a fluke," Linda said with a shrug. "That or she is a witch... but nothing special. No offence," she added in my direction. "Do you have tea? Tea would be nice."

I did some more blinking, before stepping aside and letting my 'aunts' pass. What else could I do? I needed some time to think.

"Do you have anything you might consider magical about yourself... beyond your familiar?" Minerva asked when they were sitting in the tearoom area of the apothecary and I'd offered them their choice of herbal-blended tea. "Anything at all?" she added.

"I'm good with herbs," I admitted, gesturing to the teas they were drinking. "Some people say the herbs I give them are like magic. I'm good at knowing which herbs can help people."

"What about using herbs in spells?" Minerva asked. She was trying to be subtle about it, but I knew she'd noticed the various racks of ready-made spell bags for sale on her way in.

"Everything magical you see here is for the tourists. No one from Wormwood buys them. In theory, they have all the right herbs in them to attract or repel whatever it is the user is buying them for, but... I wouldn't vouch for them being magic. They were made by Mum before..."

"They're not activated," Linda said, as if I'd meant it seriously. She turned to Minerva, as if I wasn't present. "A green witch. Really? Is that what the Salem line has come to?"

"There's nothing wrong with being a green witch! We have a cousin with those talents. He does just fine."

"Oh, sure, when the other family witches aren't hexing him for fun and calling him 'the soy witch'," Linda batted back. "She'll be bullied! She doesn't even seem to have any powers, beyond some potential intuition." She turned to me. "No offence."

"There's still time. She's not even thirty yet. It's not unheard of for a witch to come into her powers this late. Don't write her off so quickly."

"Her eyes aren't even the right colour," Linda said, visibly sulking.

"Both of you are witches..." I said, more as a statement than a question. I felt like this was a conversation I'd entered late, and now I was playing catchup.

"Yes, just like your mother was," Minerva said, a little too understandingly. She thought I was a dim bulb.

"What was she good at?" I asked, feeling all of the guilt reawaken inside of me. I'd always thought my mother was a little strange. She'd repeatedly told me I was going to grow into a fine witch one day. When I'd been older, I'd decided that it was just the Wormwood way of saying you're going to grow into a fine young woman. But if my two 'aunts' were to be believed, she had meant it more literally.

"Freya was good at everything. We hated her," Linda said, matter-of-factly.

"We did not hate her!" Minerva corrected, before turning back to me. "She was very talented at many aspects of magic."

"Which was why it was so deliciously surprising when

she ran off and got herself pregnant," Linda cut in.

"Surely someone else was also culpable for that situation," I said, dryly. Perhaps I was being pedantic, but I was the result of my mother 'getting herself' pregnant.

Minerva looked thoughtful. "Technically, you are correct, but Freya always got exactly what she wanted. It was no accident, and the fact she kept it a secret almost certainly meant it was someone who wouldn't have been approved of by the family."

"Can you blame her for not wanting to fool around with a second cousin?" Linda grimaced in my direction. "That's why Minerva's been single for forever. She won't bend the family rules, but is also not quite insane enough to pick from the list of Salem-approved suitors. No one wants a child with three eyes and tentacles. You know - because of the inbreeding," she added, completely unnecessarily.

"Why is this the first I've heard from... well... from any of my family?" I asked, still struggling to keep up.

"Freya was cut off after..." Linda gestured to me. "It's actually why..."

"...But it doesn't apply to you," Minerva interrupted. "You are not at fault for anything your mother did. The family ban on seeing you that was put in place after we met at your birth has been lifted. We are here to guide you through the time in which your powers will appear."

"Or maybe they won't," Linda added.

"But we will stay with you long enough to be sure." Minerva gifted me a smile I was certain was supposed to be reassuring.

It was not.

Silence fell for a moment, as they waited for a response from me.

I gave it to them.

"No thank you."

2

FOES AND FAKERS

The two witches exchanged a confused look.

"Pardon me?" Linda said.

"It's kind of you to come here from… wherever you came from… but I'm fine with the shop. And I don't feel magical. I'm not sure *real* magic even exists. It's far more likely to be a combination of psychological factors that lead to an outcome…"

"And what am I? A figment of your imagination?" Hemlock said from his place hiding in the shadows on one of the shelves. I ignored him. He was just a glitch in my otherwise un-magical life.

"How can she not know magic is real? She's a Salem!" Linda was talking as if I wasn't present again.

"Don't you remember? You don't notice anything supernatural until you gain your own powers. You might experience some strange things… but you know how it works. The average human mind is excellent at not seeing the truth, even when its right in front of their eyes."

"You're telling me that there's a whole world I can't see?" This entire meeting was one big magic-reveal cliché.

"Yes. It's too bad. You're really missing out," Linda said with a little shrug.

"Surely the local coven would have taken an interest in her as soon as she moved back? They would know what her last name meant," Minerva was addressing Linda again. I was seriously considering asking if they wanted me to go away whilst they ironed out the kinks in my life.

"My mother wanted me to join. I went and asked out of respect for her final wishes. They said no." Or rather, one of them in particular had said no, and her minions had merely followed her. But my 'aunts' didn't need to know the details.

"They're probably pretenders. You're better off without a coven. You've got us," Linda said. I think it was supposed to make me feel better.

"What's the high priestess like? Do you think she genuinely has some talent?" Minerva asked, something like understanding flashing across her sharp green eyes. She'd read between the lines.

"Everything seems to go right for her," I allowed - much as I hated to admit it.

"Oooh she's misusing magic." Linda looked delighted. "We could report her and get her kicked out of her coven."

"And come clean about your own crimes? I'm sure I needn't remind you why no one's heard from the Witch Council in such a long time. We have only our moral compasses to guide us... and some need more direction than others." Minerva took a sip of her tea whilst her sister eye-rolled.

"So... which room did you pick?" Linda asked, smiling brightly at me.

"The one that looks out over the garden."

"Ah, the one with the draught. Minerva had that when we were children. That was before double-glazing."

I kept my frown to myself. My 'aunts' looked like they were in their forties, at most.

"I'll take your mother's old room. She wouldn't have minded. Minerva… you can have either of the others. I don't care."

"You will not take Freya's room. That is a decision for Hazel to make. Where would you like us to go?" Minerva asked me.

I assumed that 'away' wouldn't be an acceptable response. "Either spare room is fine. I just haven't… sorted anything in Mum's room yet." It was a chore I'd managed to put off for six months already. I suspected it would wait another six.

"That sounds perfect. Thank you, Hazel. I'm sure we are going to share some wonderful times together." Minerva reached out, but thought better of it at the last moment.

"I just hope they're interesting times. When I think back to this place, the only thing that sticks out was the blanket of boredom that covered this town and strangled the life out of everything fun. Has anything changed?"

I started to automatically shake my head and then stopped. "Someone was murdered yesterday."

"How weird was the death?" Linda asked.

Even though I wasn't yet convinced I was related to this pair, they definitely knew Wormwood.

"According to the rumours, it was a ritualistic murder with occult symbols and things like that. I don't know much about the man who died, but he was a stranger to Wormwood. He had two people with him. I think they might be missing, too," I said, dredging that extra piece of information up. No one had known the names of the couple who'd allegedly accompanied the man into town, and no one I'd spoken to even had a description, beyond them being a man and a woman.

"That is unusual, even for Wormwood," Minerva

acknowledged. "I'll have to look into it, but it sounds like someone might have a bone to pick with the magical community. It's that, or you really have got a dangerous dark magician, or witch, on your hands. Someone who thinks they're powerful enough to not have to hide their practices."

"I thought the whole point of that complicated summoning and sacrifice stuff was that it was self-cleaning? Are there usually bodies left behind?" Linda asked.

"Only parts. Was this one whole?" Minerva tilted her head to one side and looked at me.

"Who **are** these people?" Hemlock muttered from his shelf.

"Yes, I think so," I said, feeling like I was falling behind again. I glanced at the clock on the wall and realised I was late opening up the shop. I got up and walked over to the glass door and flipped the sign over.

There was no big stampede through the door.

I returned to the table in the tearoom corner of the shop.

"How are things going? You haven't had the apothecary for long, have you?" Minerva tactfully enquired.

"How are you feeding yourself?" Linda seconded.

"Before all this..." I gestured around. "...I was trying to work as a writer. Non-fiction," I hastily added. As soon as you said the word 'writer', people had a tendency to start encouraging, or discouraging you, to follow your dream. Whilst I'd known many fiction writers whose earnings knocked me under the table, I'd discovered that saying you wrote fact, rather than fiction, tended to curb these kinds of conversation. "When I got back here, I started a local interest magazine. There wasn't one, and I thought it would be a good way to make money."

"Smart move. This place is hardly going to make you rich. Being a witch might help though." Linda primped her curls.

"That is breaking the rules! We are not going to be

encouraging that kind of thing," Minerva countered in that annoying habit they seemed to have of talking about me, rather than to me. I felt more like an eight-year-old than a twenty-eight-year-old.

"What are rules there for, if not to be broken?" Linda wasn't quitting.

"They're there to keep everyone safe and to make sure that things are fair. We are not having this conversation again." Minerva swivelled back to me. "Has anything come of this murder yet? Do the police have an idea of who might be behind it?"

I shook my head. "From what I've heard, it's a mystery." I considered my new-found 'aunts'. "But it could mean that Wormwood isn't a safe place for witches to be right now."

"All the more reason for us to stay here. Whoever did this, they're clearly someone dangerous. Even your name might be enough to make you a target. It sounds to me as though we've come at exactly the right time." Minerva drained the last few drops of her chamomile and lavender tea.

My ploy had just backfired spectacularly.

"Urgh, I hate this place. Why won't it just go out of business?" Linda said, before looking at me. "No offence. You could open up something nice... like a beauty parlour."

I tried to imagine a pink shop that specialised in hair and nails in the middle of Wormwood's predominately grey and grim high street. It would probably make even less money than the apothecary.

"We should get settled in. I'm sure this is all a lot for Hazel to process. Come on, Linda," Minerva said, standing up and taking her cup into the kitchen by the shop to wash it up.

"But I'm still drinking..." Linda said, looking down at her cup with regret. "Do you ever use tea leaves?"

"No." I knew what she was getting at.

She thought about it for a moment. "Good." Then she got up and followed Minerva out of the room, taking her bags with her.

I watched the pair go and stood for a long time with my hands on my hips in the middle of the shop. When I'd got up this morning, the biggest thing on my mind had been whether or not I was going to sell my packs of winter tea before they went out of date at the end of January. Now, I'd been saddled with two previously unknown aunts, who looked like they might be moving in with me for good - and it wasn't even midmorning yet! I looked down at my nearly empty cup of lemon balm and passionflower tea and lamented that it wasn't anything stronger. Sometimes flowers and herbs didn't cut it.

"I told you changes were coming," the disembodied voice called down from the shelves.

"Changes are always coming. Don't pretend you knew anything about this. It's like saying an economic crash is on its way. You know one day it's going to happen, so you'll never be wrong."

"An economic crash is coming? Excuse me. I have stocks to check on." There was a rustling sound as Hemlock disappeared somewhere else.

"I have no idea how seriously to take some of the things he says," I muttered. No matter what Hemlock claimed, I felt significantly less crazy when I was talking to myself.

I waited by the counter for a little longer. I knew that sooner or later, my regular customers would come into the shop. It wasn't the first time that I'd wondered if I was a sucker for waiting around for them... but it was the first time I closed the shop.

There was a week to go before I needed to finalise the February edition of *Tales from Wormwood*. I know... the name is hardly a work of genius, but even though I'd never fully found my specialist topic when I'd been trying to make a living as a writer, I had learned that it was important to keep your audience at the forefront of your mind, when creating a product. *Tales from Wormwood* might be a free magazine, but I made money from local businesses advertising in it. The catch was, if I didn't have a magazine that local people would want to read, no one would pay for ad space. That was why I'd had to consider my audience carefully - both when naming the magazine and when researching and writing the articles that went in it.

Most of the articles were PR pieces supplied by the local businesses themselves. I would polish them up and take a fee. But readers are smart. They know if they're just being sold to - even in a magazine they're getting for free. Every month, I had to come up with articles that engaged them and meant that when the next edition of *Tales from Wormwood* fell onto their doormat, it didn't sail straight into the bin. In some towns, sharing some nice recipes, or a heartwarming story about a local school might have done the trick. In Wormwood, it needed to be something strange.

And what better than an article covering the strange murder of Zack Baden? Part of me shrivelled up inside when I considered the way I would essentially be profiting from his death, but the journalist within said that it was news. News had to be reported, no matter how terrible it was. And as anyone who'd worked in the media industry knew - bad news was always the best news when it came to circulation numbers.

I silenced the moral protester inside of me and decided that I was going to get to the truth. It could be dicey playing with current affairs when you only published monthly, but with the deadline for printing coming up soon, I thought it was worth the risk of printing outdated news. How much could really change in a week anyway?

As I walked down Wormwood High Street, feeling strangely liberated to be skiving off shop work, I reflected that it probably wasn't even the most controversial story the magazine had ever printed. In the five months since the first issue, I'd published stories about a spectral hunter who rode a horse through Wormwood Forest, had antlers on his head, and was accompanied by the sound of rattling chains. Then there was the tale of the large bowl-shaped dip in one of the fields on the outskirts of town. According to local folklore, it had been created by a devil, trying to dig to the centre of the earth on a bet. I'd also written about a fire-spewing villain who could jump seven-feet in the air, a devil who'd once mown a local man's fields and ruined his crop, after some unwise curse words uttered by the farmer. Finally, there'd been the endless reports of UFOs, when I'd announced that the magazine was looking for other-worldly experiences. I'd hoped for stories about amazing holidays and adventures that had *felt* other-worldly... but as this was Wormwood, I'd got aliens.

The strangest thing about these tales was that they had all happened before. I'd done my research. Several similar stories cropped up across the South East of England. The difference was, whilst other towns and villages' folklore was confined to the distant past, here, a lot of people believed these things were still happening today.

Who knows? They could be correct after all, I thought to myself, considering the strange appearance of my aunts and their proclamation that I was most likely magical. I still wasn't about to tell Hemlock to hold his breath when it came to my magical powers, but the idea of a hidden world intrigued me - even though I'd never seen a single supernatural thing in Wormwood myself. I was definitely going to ask my aunts to elaborate on this 'hidden world' idea before I asked them to leave.

I sucked in some of the fresh winter air and considered my plan of action. I would need to approach the police to see what, if anything, they would tell me about the case. As they were still investigating the murder, I doubted they'd be too chatty, but there was surely some things they were approved to tell the press about. The meat of my article would be provided by the local people themselves... and I knew exactly where to start.

The Bread Cauldron Bakery was Wormwood's most successful business. It made bog-standard bread for any resident who'd miraculously managed to escape the supernatural stigma the town carried with it, but it also stocked weird, wonderful, and oh-so-very-'Wormwood' items.

I was pleased to see that the line wasn't too long at this time in the morning. The rush had already been and gone and people were sitting at the tables enjoying a coffee with their baked goods. I got to the front and ordered a lucky star biscuit (infused with lucky moonlight). Then, I got down to business.

I smiled at Tristan Coltrain, the owner of the bakery. He was new to town himself, having bought the previous failing bakery when all other suitable premises in the South East had been unaffordable. Most people who entered Wormwood that way left it just as quickly, but Tristan had embraced Wormwood's weirdness, and he had been rewarded for it. I was actually a bit jealous of his success.

"How's my favourite customer?" he said, handing over the biscuit.

"I bet you say that to all of your customers," I replied, doing my best to sparkle with charm and wit. If I ever did get my hands on some kind of magical power, I would definitely be directing it towards improving my social skills. That was totally something you could accomplish with magic, right?

"Only the ones who overpay for their biscuits when they want some juicy gossip." Tristan batted his thick eyelashes at me. "In case you're wondering... that is just you." He slid over to the side of the counter to let his assistant take over. Then he rested his chin on his hand and looked at me. "Let me guess... you want to know what I've heard about the murder."

"Wow! You should consider setting up shop as a psychic."

Tristan pulled a face. "And tangle with the psychic community in this town? No way would I go up against a group of people who can see the future. How do you win in a situation like that? They can predict your every move before you even make it." He waggled his fingers in the air.

We both knew it didn't work like that. Whilst I may still have some reservations about whether or not magic itself was actually real, I definitely believed that Wormwood's psychics were largely frauds. Comforting frauds to those who needed them, perhaps, but frauds all the same. They were people who knew how to say the right thing at the right time. But that was the extent of their 'psychic' abilities.

He brushed a strand of reddish-brown hair off his forehead. Tristan was a good looking guy. Not in the outrageous way that tended to put women off, when they considered the potential for competition, but in the accessible way that meant he was incredibly popular with the local ladies. It might also have something to do with the lack of new blood in town, when it came to finding someone you hadn't dated back in secondary school. In the past, I'd joked with him that it was his exotic face that brought the customers in, but his baking made them stay. He'd replied that if the town thought Brighton was exotic, they really needed to get out more.

I hadn't argued with him on that.

"Speaking of psychics…" Tristan said, looking around to check if anyone was listening in. (They almost certainly were.) "…I heard that Bridgette Spellsworth has been taken by the police for questioning. According to my sources, she read the dead man's fortune the night before he died, and then he, uh… didn't leave."

"He died round her house?" I said, not quite following.

"No! I mean, I suppose he might have done… I don't know. I just meant he stayed the night." He made his eyes go big with implication.

I couldn't believe I'd missed what he was saying the first time around. Bridgette Spellsworth's male dalliances were hardly headline news. It didn't surprise me at all that she'd invited a customer to stay after hours. Heck, she'd probably predicted it to him, hoping he would hang around and prove his own fortune true. There was something incredibly manipulative about that, when you paired it with a customer who wanted to believe that the fortune they'd been told was valid.

"She hasn't killed any of them before," I pointed out.

"I didn't say she did it. According to a different source, she is claiming that whilst he did stay the night, he left very early in the morning, and she had no idea at all that he'd gone."

We looked at one another.

"So… she didn't predict his death?" I said with a sideways smile on my face. You had to be careful when it came to poking fun at people in Wormwood, but Tristan had always been someone I knew didn't take any of Wormwood's weirdness seriously.

"Apparently it's a huge surprise. It's a pretty big thing to miss, isn't it? I mean… in the grand scheme of fortune telling. I know I'd want my money back if someone didn't tell me I was about to die." He grinned. "Of course - that would be a logistical nightmare, but I'd find a way. Depending on who you ask around here, ghosts are either real, or definitely real."

"Why would she kill a stranger?" I mused, wondering if Bridgette had been the one responsible for Zack Baden's death. It certainly didn't look good for her.

"I guess he probably wasn't a stranger by the time morning rolled around." Tristan waggled his eyebrows. "But I know what you mean. There aren't many people in town that I'd actually credit with murder."

I knew exactly what he meant. Like any town, most of the inhabitants were fine, but we had a few bad eggs who lurked around the place. Maybe one of them had finally exploded. "I wonder if the victim had a connection to the town… one that no one knows. He might have been here before."

Tristan shrugged. "As far as I can tell, everyone is sticking to their story that they'd never seen him before. Either it's the truth, collective amnesia, or someone is hiding something. I'm sure it will all come out in the end."

"Do you know anything about the missing people? The ones who were supposed to be with the dead man before he was…"

"…dead?" Tristan looked more amused than ever by this conversation. "All anyone seems to know is that they were a man and a woman. I haven't heard anyone give a description, even though all three of them are supposed to have been around town all day."

"Did they come into the bakery?"

Tristan's cheery expression clouded for a moment. "You know what? I think they did, but it's the strangest thing…" The smile bounced back onto his face. "…I can't remember anything about them either! It's almost like there was a lot of mist around when I saw them." He shook his head. "This place must be getting to me after all. Save yourself! Run!"

I decided to think on that some more later.

"Aurelia is looking your way," I said in an even quieter voice than the hushed tones we'd been using before.

Tristan reached across the table and grabbed my hand. "Save me."

Aurelia Ghoul was one of the higher ranking members of the coven I'd been denied entry into. She was also one of the many women in town who were after Tristan, but whilst he'd dated a few and denied the rest, she wasn't willing to quit on him.

"You brought this on yourself. Why did you go out with her?" I asked him.

"Temporary insanity? You tell me. She's a witch, right? She might have done something to me."

Usually I would have scoffed at the idea, but with two witch aunts turning up on my doorstep that morning, talking about all things magic, I wasn't as sure as I usually was.

"You're supposed to laugh," Tristan said, the alarm spreading across to him.

"Sorry. I suppose it's the murder."

My friend nodded. "It does have a way of turning a town of harmless weirdos into something more sinister. But crime happens everywhere. Wormwood is no different."

I raised my eyebrows at him.

He cringed. "Apart from the method of execution. That is where this town stands out."

I looked past him. "I think she's going to come over." I had just as much disdain for Aurelia Ghoul as I did for the high priestess of the Wormwood Coven herself. They were sisters and as thick as thieves. Wormwood's bad eggs didn't come much more rotten than the Ghouls.

"I've been meaning to ask you something... we're friends, right?" Tristan said.

"Mmhmm," I replied, looking past him to where Aurelia was shooting me daggers and sliding herself up out of her chair. I noticed she'd barely even touched the cupcake she'd bought. How did she think she'd find her way into the heart of a man who loved baking, when she clearly didn't enjoy eating it?

Is she really a witch? I wondered, thinking about everything my aunts had told me that morning. I reminded myself that I had yet to experience any signs of actual magic - even the results of magic as understood by my non-magical sensibilities, if my guests were to be believed.

There was surely no way it could be real. Otherwise, I'd be a toad at the bottom of a pond somewhere, after years of not seeing eye-to-eye with the Ghoul sisters. Recently, (thanks to a sensitive piece of information I was holding onto) we had been tolerating one another... but in the same way that nothing new ever seems to happen in town, old grudges last forever.

"...and you're single as well, so people would believe it. What do you think? Is it a stupid idea?" Tristan finished.

I realised I'd heard none of what he'd been saying. "Sorry... what?" I asked, determined to focus, even as Aurelia approached the table.

"I just think we should go out with each other officially. I want us to be serious," Tristan announced out of the blue.

I stared at him in shock. He winked at me.

I conducted some hasty guesswork regarding the parts of the conversation I'd missed.

"You're together? With **her**?" Aurelia arrived at the table right on cue.

Tristan kicked me under the table.

"Yes, we're together. We're so happy," I added, feeling that something needed to be tacked on to the end of the first statement.

Aurelia looked like she'd just been forced to lick a slug. "Seriously?" She looked me up and down before running a suggestive hand over the smug designer dress that clung to her model-slim body.

I frowned. It surely wasn't that hard to believe that Tristan could be interested in me. My hair was a nice shade of golden-brown with a natural curl to it. I had a good figure, which I kept in check by exercising in the forest (much to Hemlock's amusement). Most winningly of all, I wasn't a backstabbing *witch*.

"It's great, isn't it?" Tristan rested a hand over my shoulders.

I tried to smile and look happy. When that failed, I stuffed the rest of my biscuit in my mouth.

"We'll see how long it lasts," Aurelia said, before spinning so hard on her stiletto heel, I was surprised she didn't drill herself into the floor, and stalking straight out of the bakery. Her cupcake was left uneaten on the table where she'd left it.

"Did that sound as much like a threat to you as it did to me?" I muttered the moment I'd cleared the biscuit from my mouth.

"I'm sure she's just gone to tell everyone the happy news," he said.

"Or to put a curse on me."

Tristan didn't contradict me.

I glared at him.

"I owe you one?" he tried. When that failed to make a dent, he offered me a free box of biscuits to take home.

"I hope they really are lucky stars. I'm going to need all the luck I can get," I said, looking thoughtfully at the icing.

Tristan tapped the notice behind the counter.

· · ·

The Bread Cauldron Bakery does not offer any guarantees beyond a product that tastes truly magical!

"I hate you," I told him.

"No you don't. You're falling for me. You think I'm adorable."

I folded my arms. "How long is this ruse going to go on for?"

"As long as it takes to get everyone off my back. It will benefit us both! Don't the local men bother you all the time?"

"No." The local male population thought I was just part of the scenery… and I was happy for it to stay that way.

"Well… maybe it will help your street cred. I'll try to send customers your way. People love a budding romance."

"I'll let you know when my shop gets burned down in a mysterious arson attack."

Tristan laughed. "I can't win, can I? How about you just drop by whenever you want something baked? I'd definitely give a real girlfriend of mine all of the cakes and bread she wanted. I always have a lot left over at the end of the day anyway. To be honest, I could do with cutting down on what I eat, so it stops it from going to waste." He patted his flat abdominal muscles.

"You were doing so well until that last part," I informed him.

He slid the box across the counter and leant forwards. I hesitated for a moment before kissing him on the cheek.

"So, you want to take it slow? That's okay, sugar-pie," Tristan said, mocking me with his usual cheeky grin.

I shot him a withering look. "See you around… pumpkin pasty," I tried.

Tristan looked like he might be about to suffer a dangerous explosion of hysterical laughter.

I gathered up my lucky biscuits and waved goodbye, leaving the bakery with far more than I'd bargained for when I'd walked in.

Since waking up this morning, I'd gained two new house-mates and a fake boyfriend.

I should have known that today's strange events were far from finished.

3

SPELLS AND SHOWDOWNS

I t was almost a let down to return to the shop and find it exactly as I'd left it - with no customers in sight. If ever I'd needed a reminder of how unimportant my small business was, it was staring me right in the face.

I unlocked the door with a small sigh and walked inside to do some more sell-by date checks. At this rate, the entire shop was going to be on special offer. Perhaps I could poke my new 'boyfriend' into buying some of the herbs that needed using up, or even trading me bread in return for them.

Linda hadn't been far from the truth when she'd asked how I managed to feed myself. The answer was often from the stock I bought for the shop. With the magazine being so new, I was still trying to persuade a lot of local businesses to buy advertising space. If I were being truthful, it wasn't really enough right now. I may even have to take Tristan up on his offer to supply me with as many baked goods as I could carry.

Something needed to change... and sooner rather than later.

I was still pondering the imminent doom hovering above my head when the shop bell jangled, and a customer walked in. I looked over and readjusted my classification from 'customer' to 'nightmare'. Natalia Ghoul, the high priestess of the Wormwood Coven, had just walked in to my shop.

I gritted my teeth and prepared for the worst. Not only was Natalia the one who'd denied me entry, on the basis that I was a dud witch, she also happened to be the older sister of Aurelia. She must have taken the theft of Tristan even harder than I'd thought, if she was already sending her sister in to sort me out.

"What can I do for you?" I asked, brightly. I was not going to be the one to cast the first stone.

However, I was secretly hoping my magical aunts would materialise and put some of their 'powers' to good use. If they could turn Natalia into a frog, that would definitely convince me magic was real.

"Do you have any blue vervain, dill, and dittany of Crete?" she asked in a superior manner that hinted she doubted I had any of it.

I fetched all of the pots down and then asked her how much of each item she would like.

"Oh, you know... enough." Her eyes glittered when she said it. "What am I saying? You probably don't even know what I'm talking about! How silly of me to forget that you're not really a witch."

I looked her straight in the eye. "I may not be a witch, but I do own an apothecary in Wormwood. I know what those herbs are for."

"But do you know *who* they're for?" The glitter turned into a glint of malice.

I made a mental note to tell Tristan to search all of his pockets and not eat or drink anything that he hadn't prepared himself.

"That is your business. I just sell the herbs." I measured a reasonable amount of each out, and then added more when Natalia snapped at me. I made the changes with pleasure. If the high priestess thought she could alarm me with the amount of love-spell herbs she was willing to throw into this obvious ploy to get even, she was sorely mistaken. I totted up the total cost with pleasure. It would probably be the most money I earned all day.

"Oh, by the way... you remember a couple of weeks ago when you ordered in that thing for me? The items you sell to customers are confidential, right?" Natalia casually dropped in, at the same time she dropped the money from a great height into my hand.

"The mandrake root?" I asked. That had been a special order. I stocked a number of mildly poisonous plants, which were commonly used in things like hexes, and even in the fake tourists' charms I sold, but when it came to substances that could actually do real damage, I had to be careful what I supplied.

Being a witch supply shop, I had to bend a few rules, or risk losing customers. Poisonous plants were fairly easy to get around. For example, the government list of banned and restricted herbal ingredients included one variety of mandrake (Mandragora autumnalis) but there were several other types, which shared similar properties, but weren't yet included on the banned list. Even so, I always made my customers sign a form where they promised that I'd sold them toxic plants as a curiosity, rather than for actual use. I doubted anyone would sue me, given that they had to know that I wasn't a worthwhile target in terms of money, but it felt professional to cover the eventuality. You never knew when it might save your skin.

"Yes... that order," Natalia confirmed, her eyes darting left and right. "You won't tell anyone?"

I frowned, sensing a trap. "Is there something I need to know before making a promise like that?" I dangled the prospect of my silence like a carrot, to see if she would bite.

"No. I just like my affairs to be kept private. You would be a pretty shoddy businesswoman if you broke the code of confidentiality." She flicked a strand of auburn hair back from her collar and scrunched up her annoyingly pretty nose.

"I'm a business owner, not a medical professional. I don't gossip about what customers purchase, but if I am ever asked to share information that might pertain to a legal situation... I would of course comply." I watched Natalia carefully when I said it.

Right on cue, colour rose up her neck.

"I think that's disgusting. I'm sure the police will be equally interested to hear about why you're supplying illegal substances!" The explosion had been immediate. I didn't fail to notice that she'd mentioned the police. That was interesting.

"The police are welcome to look into my business practices, if they choose," I said, as mildly as I could.

In truth, I was a little worried. My shop operated in a grey area of the law, and I wasn't sure how my disclaimers and work arounds would appear if they did decide to take an interest.

Natalia's hand tightened on the paper bags of herbs, and for a second, I imagined she might be about to throw the lot in my face. Fortunately, it was at that precise moment my newfound aunts walked through from the kitchen into the shop.

"Good afternoon," Minerva began, smiling in true shop-keeper fashion. The smile dropped when she seemed to see Natalia properly for the first time.

What happened next was... weird.

Both Linda and Minerva tilted their heads and squinted at Natalia, whilst the high priestess attempted to do the same... and then seemed to look flustered. Dare I say it - even a bit panicked.

I was so busy enjoying the strange effect my aunts were having on a woman I found loathsome that I almost missed the sudden change in air pressure, as something invisible seemed to rush by.

"You're a charmer, aren't you?" Linda's eyes flashed with amusement.

Natalia looked terrified. I sensed it took every ounce of her dignity to spin on her heel and march out of the shop.

The moment she was gone, I turned to my house guests. "What was that?"

"You didn't see it? Oh, of course you didn't," Minerva said, tilting her head apologetically.

"I saw it. It was nothing to write home about," a superior voice came from on top of the shelves.

I ignored it. I wasn't even sure I believed that Hemlock could see anything I couldn't. At least... he'd never mentioned it before now.

"Hazel, do you know that witch?" Minerva continued.

"She's the high priestess of the local coven."

My guests exchanged a significant look.

"We'll see about that," Linda said, with the kind of reassuring smile a ferociously protective mother gives to her child, before personally beating up their school bully.

"No need to put yourselves out," I told them with an easy smile. Seeing Natalia get... whatever it was that had happened to her... had been more than enough excitement for me.

"Hardly," Linda said, shooting an amused look at her sister. "Jumped up little witch. She must barely be..."

Minerva silenced her sister with a wave of her hand, so suddenly that it might have been magic.

I felt a surprising rush of frustration bubble up inside me. "Will I ever be able to see it?" I asked, before I could stop myself. Was I really jumping on this crazy bandwagon of believing in magic - actual magic?

"We'll see," Linda said, recovering her powers of speech. "Ha! See what I did there?"

"Give it time. You are still young. Try not to worry about it. Even if you don't have our family's magical gifts, you'll still lead a fulfilled life." Minerva lifted her hands and looked around the shop.

I crossed my arms. She had got to be kidding.

"I can see that you have a lot to do. We won't keep you any longer. Let us know if you have any trouble at all with that other witch," Minerva said, before turning and walking back into the kitchen. "Come on, Linda."

"Why? She doesn't look busy."

"Linda!"

"Fine." My aunt dutifully trotted after her sister.

"And fix your hair colour! It's ridiculous, and it will all fall out, if you're not careful..." I heard before they passed out of earshot.

Hemlock jumped down onto the counter. "Did you feel that back there? There was so much power in here it made my whiskers sizzle."

"Stop looking at me like that," I told him, tidying away the last few scraps of spilled love-spell herbs.

"Like what?"

"Like you're wishing I would do something interesting. Something magical."

"*They* seem to think you will do one day. For what it's worth, I think you will, too..."

I reached a hand out to stroke his chin.

"… because there's no way my talents would be wasted on a loser!" he finished.

I withdrew the hand. "Hey!"

"But seeing as you're still looking distinctly normal today, I think I'll get a manicure to pass the time." Hemlock trotted off, chortling to himself under his breath.

"I hope it blunts your claws!" I called after him, much too late. It wasn't much of a comeback. *Is this what things have come to? Losing arguments to a cat?* I thought, suddenly feeling down about everything.

I told myself to knock it off and looked on the bright side. Natalia had been rattled by my aunts. Perhaps she wouldn't be so keen to get even with me over the little disagreement we'd had regarding client confidentiality - not when she believed I was under their protection. It would appear that I had discovered an upside to my new housemates. But it wasn't enough to stop me from finding them somewhere else to stay.

It wasn't that I didn't believe that these two glamorous women with their aura of power weren't really my aunts, but…

No.

Wait.

That was it.

I wasn't convinced that they were my aunts.

And until I could get to the bottom of whatever was going on here, they would have to stay somewhere else. With the recent murder and the killer (or killers) still at large, it seemed unwise to harbour a couple of strangers in my house. That was why I found myself waiting in the waiting room of Grant Kingsley's impressive residence the next morning.

Grant was Wormwood's most well-known landlord. He owned the majority of rented property in the area and had been a long-time resident - the same as almost everyone else in town. I was hoping that he would have somewhere suitable for my aunts to rent until I established some facts about who they really were, and why they were in town. It was only now that I considered I didn't know what kind of thing they could afford. Or if they could afford anything at all.

Oh well. It cost nothing to find out about some potential properties. Then I'd just suggest the possibility to my aunts and hope they didn't hex me.

It was a totally foolproof plan.

I stood up from the leather seat I'd been directed to and wandered around the room. Grant's success spoke for itself. His large manor house on the hill overlooking town had been decorated in a monochrome palette that added a modern feel to the traditional rooms. I tilted my head and wondered if I could get away with the dove grey shade this room had been painted in the cottage I'd inherited. After a moment of reflection, I decided that this place got away with its cutting-edge style because of the room-size. My little cottage needed to keep its cosy pastel palette.

I was admiring the chromed stag-head when I heard someone walk into the room.

"Hazel Salem?"

I turned to see Grant Kingsley approaching with his hand outstretched.

I shook it and smiled at him.

"To what do I owe the pleasure? I was under the impression that you owned your own property." He beckoned me to follow him out of the room and down the corridor beyond it. "Is the business not treating you well? I am always looking to expand my portfolio…"

"Business is fine," I said, a little too quickly. "I'm here to

38

ask if you have any residential properties available to rent. I have some... guests... staying with me at the moment, and I think they might want to extend their stay indefinitely."

Grant's eyebrows immediately shot up. I didn't blame him. Anyone wanting to move in to Wormwood was a rare thing. The landlord rubbed his salt and pepper stubble whilst he thought.

Grant Kingsley was considered hot property to the slightly more mature ladies of Wormwood. He had a pleasant face, accented by sharp brown eyes, and a jawline that hadn't yet gone jowly. He also came complete with his own property empire. I could appreciate the appeal. Much to the locals' sorrow, Grant Kingsley had remained a bachelor for as long as I could remember. There was speculation over this, but I hadn't heard any theory that quite rang true, when I considered the man holding the door open for me to walk into his office.

"Do you know a budget?" he asked, as I'd known he would.

"I was hoping you could give me a range of things to show my guests. I don't actually know much about them."

The eyebrows were raised yet further. "Of course! I think Julie's got a few portfolios stashed away somewhere. I'll be right back..." He turned in the doorway and walked away down the corridor to find the secretary who'd let me in.

Grant Kingsley had a reputation for getting through secretaries. This habit just added fuel to the fire of one of the theories about Grant's perpetual bachelor status, but I didn't think it was the correct answer. Whilst the woman I'd met when I'd entered the residence had been fairly young and pretty, she'd also looked as though she'd be more likely to tap dance on hot coals than break her air of professionalism. When I added that to Grant's own lack of warmth towards everyone and anyone, it didn't make for fireworks.

I swivelled on the chair in front of the desk, enjoying the opportunity to have a nose into someone else's life. Grant's office had been painted in a light off-white colour. It was clinical and probably designed to make you stop looking at the walls and get some work done. His desk was the focal point of the room. It was a huge thing, made from sleek, dark wood, and it was busy-looking without being messy.

I glanced back towards the door and then stood up to take a closer look at what had been left on the desk. I saw big sheets of impressive-looking modern property development plans and photos of properties I knew that Grant owned in Wormwood... and some that I didn't, but I wasn't surprised. If you were looking for a landlord in town, he had the monopoly. I don't know what I'd hoped to see whilst spying on his work - a love letter to a person he'd been having a secret affair with for all these years? I was just as bad as the gossips in town.

I wound my neck in just in time for Grant to return.

He handed me a couple of glossy folders. "There you go. That should give your guests a good range of prices and property types to start their search with. Do let me know if there's anything more I can do to help."

"Thank you," I said, nodding to him. I stood up to go, before remembering that I was supposed to be writing an article... an article that I badly needed to flesh out with local opinions. "I hate to ask, but has your business been affected by that terrible murder? I can't believe something like that happened in Wormwood!" I winced at my own words, knowing that it was the standard phrase you rolled out whenever something bad happened in your town. If I were being truly honest, I'd have said it was actually surprising that more people hadn't turned up dead. Or at least - been found dead.

"It was only a matter of time," Grant said, echoing my

own thoughts. "A section of our town suffers from a mass delusion. The rest of us have tolerated it for as long as I can remember, but it's always been like leaving a pot on the boil. Sooner or later, it's going to spill over."

I nodded, knowing I was supposed to agree with him.

"It was only a matter of time before the silliness got out of hand," he said, echoing his earlier statement. "I wish there were more sensible people in town. I know your mother went in for all of that stuff, but you're different, aren't you?"

I discovered I didn't know whether to nod or shake my head. I settled for an attempt at a smile.

He nodded, reassuring me that I'd given the right response. "You shouldn't pander to them, you know. I understand that you were left that shop by your mother and that it's been in your family for generations... but everything comes to an end. Sometimes change is a good thing. You should give me a call, if you ever want to sell the shop. I know it's not your passion."

That was typical Grant - buttering people up so that they would sell him the properties he had his eye on. I knew that shops tended to be lucrative for landlords - even shops in Wormwood. Mine was one of only a couple that weren't owned by the property tycoon.

"I'll definitely consider it," I said to appease him. I also said it to keep my options open. I was painfully aware that the shop wasn't making pots of money... and neither was my writing. I had bills to pay and a future to think about.

"You must agree that this witchcraft is all utter nonsense. I've said it for years and now look what happens! Someone takes it too seriously and we have something that negatively impacts the entire town." He ran a hand through his wavy black and grey hair. I knew he was thinking about the local property prices and their rental value. "I just hope the police can wrap it up soon and put away whoever is responsible.

With a bit of luck, it will teach some of the people around here that they're encouraging unhinged behaviour. Fairytales and make believe are something that any normal adult leaves behind in their childhood."

"Do you think someone in town killed the victim?" I asked, curious to know if Grant believed that it was a Wormwooder, or some outside affair that had leeched into town.

"I've no idea. We have our bad apples like any place," he said, echoing my own thoughts once again. He rubbed his chin. "You know... for a bunch of fortunetellers, you wouldn't believe how often my rent payments are late, due to unforeseen circumstances. Can you believe that?" He shrugged his shoulders and grinned before it faded away, as another thought occurred to him.

"If I were the police, I'd be looking at the people running around claiming to help their customers do nasty things to other people. If they're willing to sell a service like that, what does that say about them? Maybe someone didn't pay them on time, and they thought they'd deal out a little punishment of their own." He shook his head. "If the ego gets big enough..."

I didn't have to ask who he was talking about.

While there were a few people about town I was wary around (I'd fallen out with two such people in the past twenty-four hours) there was one person who had them all beaten, when it came to bad magic.

"Let me know about the houses..." Grant said, waving a hand my way and looking suddenly distracted by the work on his desk.

I knew how to take a hint. This particular interview was over.

I walked out of Grant Kingsley's house with an armful of rental properties and a new murder suspect.

4

A NASTY PIECE OF WORK

Hellion Grey was a nasty piece of work.

He made no secret of it either. It was even written on his business cards. He inhabited a property at the end of one of Wormwood High Street's dark lanes that led to nowhere. In most towns, Hellion would have made the local news when he'd decided to paint the entire building black, but no one had batted an eyelid here. The shop window below the flat was filled with an assortment of nasty things - voodoo dolls, inverted religious symbols, and evil-looking tomes. A hand-lettered sign in the glass read: Hellion Grey, High Magician and Demon Summoner. Below that, there was a quote in cursive writing:

Got a nasty piece of work you want taken care of? Let an even nastier piece of work do it for you! Get revenge. Get what you want. Get even.

I stood in the lane outside of the shop whilst the last rays of winter light were sucked away by the great dark building, and reflected that I concurred with the landlord's implied suspicions. If ever there was a prime candidate for a twisted, ritualistic killer, it was Hellion Grey.

It was only now that I was standing outside his shop that I realised pointing that fact out to him might not be in my best interests. Especially if he really was responsible.

I needed to come up with a plausible excuse for being here. My mind turned blank... just as the door was opened wide.

Hellion Grey smiled out at me, his gold tooth glinting in the dying light. "Ms Salem. I can't say I'm surprised to see you here today."

"You're not?" I said, and then tried to look mysterious and not flummoxed.

He inclined his head. "It takes a wise person to know the mind of their enemies... and to make their enemies' attack dog a better offer." He raised his hairy brown eyebrows suggestively.

"Which enemy in particular are we talking about?" I enquired.

"A woman with many enemies! They say that's the true sign of an interesting person." He flipped his long gold and black sleeves back with a flourish and indicated that I should enter his domain. I would rather have cosied up with a scorpion, but I refused to back out now. I wanted to get the inside story. Sometimes, being the first to know the truth meant taking a few risks. The way things were going right now, a great story in *Tales from Wormwood* might be the difference between having electricity and not having electricity next month.

I walked past Hellion Grey and entered his lair.

"So... what are we thinking? A well-placed curse? How severe do you want to go? Once we have reached an agreement, I'll be happy to tell you what your not-so-good friend picked out for you." His eyes glittered as he ran a hand down a row of distorted glass jars. Inside were all manner of things. Various pickled animals floated in eternal suspension, a jar of dried beetles sparkled like dark gemstones, and I recognised several dried herbs that were definitely on the banned poisons list. He hadn't got those from me, that was for sure. All things considered, I was glad that Hellion Grey hadn't given me his business. Just being here was giving me the willies.

"What's to stop you from returning to your original employer and double-crossing me the way you're double-crossing them?" I asked, feigning an interest in a jar of grey dirt - probably taken from a graveyard. I knew this display was supposed to impress me - scare me, even - but I didn't really believe in any of this ominous magic stuff he was peddling. I believed in Hellion Grey least of all. I would only consider him a threat if I saw him holding a knife. I looked out of the corner of my eye at the rack filled with ceremonial knives for sale. I'd definitely come to the right place.

"You're an intelligent young witch, aren't you?" He was laying it on thick. I wondered how much money he thought he was going to squeeze out of me today. He would be sorely disappointed to learn of my limited funds.

"I'm not a witch," I replied automatically.

The eyebrows went higher. "Oh? You could have fooled me."

I allowed my mouth to quirk up on the side that was facing away from the black magic practitioner. The conversation was going my way. "It's becoming a dangerous thing to go around telling people you're a witch. I'm not as talented as you. I wouldn't be able to defend myself. That terrible murder has made people worry about our beloved supernatural community." I turned and tilted my head at him. "I don't like to overstep, but you're an expert in ritual magic, aren't you? Do you have a professional opinion on what was done to the poor man who was murdered? I'm just so worried about all of this..." Now I was the one laying it on thick.

But it worked. Hellion's face creased with sympathy. "My dear Ms Salem! There is no need to worry for our community's safety. I know the way the local witches work, and it was no act of witchcraft that ended in that man's death. It was murder, pure and simple. It's too bad that the simple, closed minds of those investigating this terrible crime can't see it for what it is - an insult to all of us." He raised a hand. "I'm not saying it wasn't done by a resident of this town, but it certainly wasn't magically motivated. It is my belief that this problem will not be troubling us for an undue length of time. The resident responsible has been apprehended and all-but arrested, according to my sources." Hellion looked smug for a moment.

"Do you mean Bridgette? You think she actually did it?"

Hellion gave his satin-clad shoulders a little shrug. "It makes sense. The fortunetellers and we real magic practitioners have always been at odds. She must have been more ambitious than anyone realised, setting us all up like that. I understand why she chose to make it appear as if I myself had something to do with the unfortunate death, but even a blindman would notice the inconsistencies. What happened in the woods is the equivalent of a four-year-old attempting to produce a copy of a Monet." He shook his head. "And look where it's got her! I always warn my clients... don't attempt anything you're not qualified to do. Toying with the forces of darkness is a sure-fire way of getting something bad attached to you. Ms Spellsworth is finding that out to her cost. If she'd really wanted to achieve something productive with that murder, she should have come to me for help."

I blinked. Had he really just hinted that he was A-okay

with assisting murder? I was still wondering how to plumb these new depths when the creepy man walked towards me, waving his hands threateningly in the air.

I ducked and debated darting backwards to grab one of the ceremonial knives.

"Stop moving around! You have dark energies clinging all over you. They're tricky. It took me a while to see them... but they're there." He flapped around my head. "They don't want to let you go. What have you been up to? This is most irregular."

"My aunts just moved in?" I couldn't think of anything else to say.

"Witches, are they? Hmmm. Perhaps that's it," Hellion didn't look convinced. "Have they performed any recent acts of magic?"

"There was a little disagreement with Natalia Ghoul."

Hellion's expression was immediately alert. It looked like I wouldn't need any extra cash to find out the family responsible for trying to curse me. My best guess was that Aurelia was shooting for success in two directions. She'd dispatched Natalia to put together a love spell for Tristan... and I was getting a curse.

"There could have been some kind of energetic overspray, I suppose," he concluded, before turning away to pace back up the room.

I took the opportunity to pull a face at *that* gross expression.

"We were talking about curses, weren't we?" the high magician said, gathering his senses again. "What kind of curse might you want to put on your enemy? I can make some really nasty things happen. If you need any inspiration, just wait until you hear what she had planned for you!"

"I think we were talking about reassurances that you're not a double-crosser... even though you're double-crossing a client right now," I batted back, knowing I was walking a thin line.

"I wouldn't insult your intelligence."

"But you would Aurelia's?" This time, the twitch was unmissable. It had been Aurelia herself who'd come running to Hellion to make me sorry for stealing her man. "I think I'll take my chances, if it's all the same to you." I wasn't going to be caught in some ridiculous bidding war with an unscrupulous bad guy. I knew the price would keep going up. I probably didn't even have enough cash to fulfil Hellion's standard price for his services. Not cash that I could spare, anyway.

Hellion's customer-pleasing expression vanished. In its place was a sly middle-aged man, who looked like he slithered rather than walked. "I suggest you reconsider. A witch like Aurelia might be able to do something to take the edge off my work… but I hear you're a dud."

So much for 'one of us', I silently observed. "True. But my aunts aren't. They're both proper Salems, and they're here to protect me until I develop my own powers." I borrowed a trick from Natalia and tried to look haughty and superior.

"Aren't you a little on the old side? Unless…" He shook his head. "I suppose we'll see what they're made of. You'd better warn them there's a storm coming."

"You're the one who should be worried," I told him, whilst silently wondering if I were in any position at all to be making threats. My aunts had certainly looked impressive when they'd seen off Natalia, but I didn't have a clue as to what they'd really done, or even how good they were at whatever it was they did. Half of me still believed we were talking about fairytales, rather than real life. If they hadn't come to town, I'd probably have laughed at Hellion's threats and watched as absolutely nothing happened.

I might have drunk some anti-curse sage tea with a dash of rue in it. Just in case. But that would have been the full extent of my preventative actions. Psychology was what I'd believed magic relied upon to work, and I would never have given this twisted man the satisfaction.

But now I wasn't so sure. Perhaps it was the body in the woods with its dark symbols, or maybe it was my aunts' whispered words about magical powers, but I was rattled. Ironically, I knew that made me more vulnerable to Hellion's work than ever before. If magic was real, I hoped my aunts were darn good at it. After a moment's consideration, I decided I'd file the folders for rental properties I'd collected from Grant Kingsley. What was wrong with a little family time spent together fighting off curses?

"We'll see about that," Hellion said, touching his fingertips together and lowering his head. I waited for the inevitable super-villain cackle.

Instead, I was treated to the sound of breaking glass as an object crashed through the shop window, narrowly missing me.

We both looked at the rock-shaped object on the shop floor.

I bent down and picked it up.

It was a rock.

But there was something tied around it.

"Love letter from a secret admirer?" I sniped, unwrapping the paper to see what it read.

"Give me that! I'm the one it was addressed to!" Hellion jumped up and down, but - like an alarmingly high proportion of evil men - he was short. I kept it out of his reach with ease.

"You call something being thrown through the window an addressed item?"

"It's not the first time it's happened..." he muttered, before resuming his ridiculous jumping around. I could almost feel the as-yet-unperformed curse becoming less effective by the jump. This man was a clown.

"It's a hate note. No surprises there, I suppose?" I told him, reading the words scrawled in capitals on the scrap of paper. "It's a request for you to leave town now, or die. It also calls you a witch… but it's meant as an insult. I assume the writer wants to imply that they will be the one to kill you. That's not been made incredibly clear, has it? They should have thought about it more before committing it to a rock."

"I don't need a literary review of my death threat!" Hellion protested. I lowered my hand and let him snatch away the paper and rock. I lamented the fact I hadn't seen the identity of the person who'd done the throwing before they'd run away.

I'd have liked to buy them a drink.

Whilst Hellion was still poring over the note and muttering curses under his breath that may, or may not, have had any magical bearing, I took the opportunity to leave the little shop of horrors. With a bit of luck, the crazy magician would be more hung up on his own problems than those of Aurelia Ghoul.

When I walked back down the street, tracing the path of the mystery window-breaker, my eyes jumped to every moving shadow. I may be no further towards uncovering the truth about the circumstances surrounding the death of Zack Baden, but I knew one thing for sure. Wormwood was starting to boil over. If someone didn't do something to solve this murder, and fast, it would be out of the cauldron and into the fire.

5

THE PLAGUE OF WORMWOOD

The next place my evening's investigation took me to was Bridgette Spellsworth's cottage. If there was a storm brewing in Wormwood, then she was surely at its centre. Bridgette lived close to the edge of town. Her cottage was one that I knew had been passed down through the generations, the same as the apothecary in my own family. Unlike Hellion's gaudy advertisements, the only symbol that Bridgette's house was anything other than a home was the tasteful wooden sign at the bottom of her garden that advertised her services as a traditional fortuneteller.

Or it had done, before someone had sprayed the word 'witch' across it in black spray paint. I frowned at the sign. If the vandal had written 'killer' I wouldn't have been surprised, but when I paired the use of 'witch' with the window-smashing at Hellion's place, I was definitely starting to sense a trend. Bridgette's boarded up windows further confirmed my theory that people were taking their own action against those they perceived culpable for the crimes committed in the forest.

I walked up the garden path, pausing only to look at the missing persons posters that had been pasted on top of the boarded up windows. I doubted anyone would be finding the people pictured. Instead of a photo, two generic grey shapes of a man and woman had been used. There was no accompanying description and no mention of any names. For all intents and purposes, the two people, who'd allegedly come into town at the same time as the murder victim, were ghosts.

I wonder if the police have found out anything about them? I thought, and then I wondered if the police had found out anything at all. Hellion had said that Bridgette had been all-but arrested by the police, but she hadn't actually been arrested. That probably meant they didn't believe, or didn't have the evidence that she'd done it.

I rang her bell and then knocked on the door. With the windows boarded up, it was impossible to tell if the lights were on inside. When I pressed my ear to the door, I thought I heard the sound of someone scuttling away, but no one answered. I stepped back from the little porch and realised I didn't blame Bridgette for not rushing to open the door to an unexpected visitor. She would have seen what had been done to her sign, and the broken glass underneath her boarded up windows told their own story. Bridgette Spellsworth didn't need to be a fortuneteller to know that people thought she'd killed a man.

I put thoughts of my magazine article to one side and decided to leave Bridgette alone. I couldn't imagine what she must be going through at the moment. Deep down, I knew I didn't really believe she'd done it. People said it was the quiet and unassuming ones you had to watch out for, but Bridgette had never struck me as malicious. Sure, she had her enemies. We had that in common with each other. But I'd sold the fortuneteller herbs in the past, and I'd been able to guess what she'd used them for. Whether or not they worked, I had no idea, but I did know that Bridgette's idea of revenge was petty. The thought of her sacrificing a customer she'd asked to stay the night to some unknown terrible force, and then leaving the body lying out in the open displayed like that, felt all kinds of wrong.

Something was going on in Wormwood right now. But I wasn't convinced it was as simple as black magic.

The streets were silent when I trudged back through them to my little shop. Upon reflection, they were probably a little too silent. I stopped wallowing in self-pity over my financial problems long enough to take a good look around.

I wasn't disappointed.

On every streetlamp, a headless rat or pigeon had been tied around the pole. Each small body had been impaled with evil-looking pins, and you'd have to be living in a box to not recognise the satanic symbols scrawled, horror-movie style, over each corpse. It was awful. It was gross. If it were in a modern gallery, we'd probably call it art.

I took a step closer to one of the headless pigeons.

"It's real. I already checked," a voice came from down by my feet. "Fresh, too. Finger-lickin' good, if you ask me."

I shuddered. "I don't suppose you happened to see who did it?" I asked my wayward familiar.

"Nope. I was busy."

"Doing what?" Hemlock's idea of 'busy' usually meant he'd been messing with stuff. My stuff.

"Wouldn't you like to know…" He did that annoying smug run with his tail bolt upright in the air - the one that cats do when they know they've just got away with something.

"Hemlock, wait! Do you see any dark energies around me? Hellion said he saw something."

"What were you doing talking to that loser? He probably

said it to scare you into buying something from him. What did he do next, try to sell you a curse?"

"Maybe," I confessed. "I didn't buy anything. Someone threw a rock through the window."

"I bet that happens a lot."

"You know, he did say something along those lines…"

"Did you get anything good for the article? At least the rock will add some drama. You're going to need it. I've read your articles before."

"What article? And hey! I'm a great writer. A good writer," I amended, losing confidence as soon as I said it.

"The article you're writing about this murder. It doesn't take a detective to work out why you paid a visit to the man who hears all of the town's gossip, and then took a trip to the nastiest magical maniac in Wormwood. It's a good thing you're not the killer. The police would have joined the dots in minutes with the trails you leave. Speaking of the police, they're waiting in the shop for you."

I ground to a halt. "What?! Why didn't you tell me?"

"I just did." Hemlock looked smugger than ever.

"I meant why didn't you tell me *before*?" I gritted my teeth and wondered if having Hemlock neutered would curb his smart aleck behaviour. No one would argue that he hadn't had it coming.

"I figured it wasn't that urgent. Your aunts are with them, so it's fine."

It was about as far from fine as you could get.

"Hemlock!" I sped up my walk to a trot.

"What? I like them. They gave me a whole can of cat food instead of half. You're stingy."

"You don't need a whole can. And stop forming opinions on people by the amount of food they bribe you with. You're so shallow."

I could see the shop now. It was still standing and nothing looked broken. That was hopefully a good sign.

"*I'm* shallow? I'm not the one selling herself out with a fake boyfriend in return for biscuits. At least get some money out of it like a proper working... heyyy!"

I enjoyed the blessed silence that descended after I picked Hemlock up and tossed him into the large bin next to the shop. It was only then that I remembered the apothecary was supposedly crawling with police, and I'd just committed what would probably appear like a terrible act of animal cruelty to an innocent observer.

"I'll get you for this! You can't just shut me... oooh fish heads..."

I left Hemlock to his bin diving and made a mental note to not let him on my bed later. Or actually anywhere in the house at all.

I made sure that I walked into the apothecary the way I normally would and looked suitably surprised to find a cluster of people waiting inside for me.

"Hazel Salem, I presume?" A man stepped forwards from the small group. I noticed that they were all drinking speciality teas that I doubted they'd pay for. I would have to have words with my aunts about hospitality tea, versus premium products with things called 'activated herbs'. I consoled myself that if the teas really did work, perhaps some of the officers would come back for more.

"Where have you been?" he continued when I inclined my head to indicate my identity.

I focused my attention on the man addressing me. He was in his thirties and not dressed in a uniform, which I presumed meant he outranked his companions. His white shirt was crisp and clean and did little to cover the broad chest and shoulders it contained. The hint of aftershave I smelled when he approached spoke of lime and the heart of the woods. It was an intriguing mix. I raised my gaze to meet his grey eyes and saw curiosity reflected back at me. Was he as intrigued by me as I was by him?

Hang on. He'd asked me a question. And I was completely ignoring it. That was probably the cause of his curiosity. I opened my mouth to give an honest answer. I hesitated, remembering exactly what I'd been up to. These members of the police force were surely here to ask questions pertaining to the recent murder. When you looked at it in a certain way, I knew my evening spent hanging out with a black magic practitioner, my visit to the prime suspect's house, and then my walk through a row of animal corpses (with no one around to witness it) might be regarded as suspicious.

But do you know what was even more suspicious? Hesitating before answering what should have been a simple question.

"I'm sorry, I'm just a bit shaken," I said, deciding to run with part of the truth. "On my way back here, I came across something really horrible. Someone has killed some rats and pigeons and strung them to the lampposts out in the street. I think it could be the same person who killed the man in the forest," I confessed. That much certainly seemed likely if the description of the scene of the crime I'd been hearing about was correct. This killer had a certain style.

"Dobbs and Benson. Investigate this report," the man said, signalling to the two officers waiting in the shop with a flick of his wrist. He kept his eyes on me the whole time he said it. I could almost sense him searching for guilt and blood-stained hands. I tried to cast a surreptitious glance downwards.

Oh great. There was blood on my hands. I'd picked up Hemlock to throw him into the bin after he'd told me he'd snacked on one of the pigeons. I clamped my hands shut and hoped I'd been the first to notice.

"We'll leave you to talk in private," Minerva said, tugging on Linda's arm when she didn't immediately move.

"Ohhhh," Linda complained, but she left the room with a reluctant backwards glance in the direction of the man I was talking to.

"Sorry, but… who are you?" I asked the man in front of me, hoping to deflect his questioning for a little longer while I gathered my thoughts, lies, and alibis.

"I'm Detective Sean Admiral of the Witchwood Police Force," he said, never taking his eyes off me.

I supposed it made sense that the murder case had been passed on to them. Witchwood was the largest nearby town. Wormwood didn't even have a police station. "Are you here to investigate the murder?"

"Yes. I have some questions I would be grateful if you were able to answer."

"I'd be happy to," I said, hoping that things were heading along a more predictable track now that we'd started over.

"Before we begin, would you mind telling me where you were this evening? I spoke to your aunts, but they weren't aware of your whereabouts." Detective Admiral looked perplexed by my lack of foresight in failing to let my aunts know where I was at all times.

"I only found out that I have aunts today," I said, hoping that the confusion that would cause would distract from the next thing I was about to admit to. "I wasn't doing much. I visited Hellion Grey to talk to him about his views on the murder case. He supposedly specialises in ritual magic. Then, I tried to visit Bridgette Spellsworth, but she didn't answer her door. On my way back, I saw what had been done to the lampposts." I knew better than to lie about where I'd been. Even though every street I'd walked down had been silent and empty, a lot of people watched from windows. And a lot of people gossiped.

"You went to ask about the murder? Why?" the detective asked, as I'd known he would.

"I own and write the local interest magazine. Whilst tragic, the murder is a big story. The magazine could really do with a readership boost..." I said, as apologetically as I could. I knew what I was doing was morally questionable, but it was only what newspapers did every day.

"I'm sure I don't have to explain to you that interfering in a police investigation is an offence."

I frowned. "I'm not interfering! I'm not even investigating. I'm just interviewing."

The detective threw me a disbelieving look. He looked all the more attractive for it.

"I'm not sure it's wise to be poking around a murder investigation when you yourself might be implicated. We came here today to enquire about the sale of an illegal substance believed to have been sold on these premises."

"Which illegal substance?" I naively asked, before regretting it. "I mean... I don't sell anything illegal, to my knowledge." Yep. I was doing a bang-up job of coming across as completely innocent. No one was going to doubt my story for a second.

Something twitched in the detective's eye. "Dried mandrake root. Forensics believe it was used to poison the deceased, prior to his death. It might have been administered to incapacitate him to make the execution simpler. Do you sell mandrake root?"

"Not usually," I said, thinking about Natalia's strange visit, and her even stranger request to me to keep silent about what I'd sold her. It was all starting to make sense now.

"But you have sold some recently?"

"I did, but it wasn't the illegal kind. Technically, the law only pertains to one variety of what is commonly referred to as mandrake. I sell a different type."

"Did you not stop to wonder why someone might be buying mandrake root?" The detective was giving me a look that said he doubted my mental faculties.

"With all due respect, you aren't from Wormwood, are you, Detective? A lot of people buy a lot of strange things for a multitude of different reasons. I just sell what people will buy."

"Spoken like a true drug dealer," the detective said, dryly, but he looked sorry he'd let it slip a second later. He'd let his professionalism get away from him.

I decided to help him out by throwing him a bone. "Mandrake root has a rich history of varying uses. In the Bible it was used to help Rachel conceive Jacob. In Greek mythology Aphrodite and Circe are alleged to have used it as an aphrodisiac. The root was also used as an anaesthetic in ancient Roman times. It has hallucinogenic and narcotic properties, which made it a fairly appropriate choice, but if you took too much…"

"…you wound up dead," the detective completed, not looking reassured by the information I was freely giving.

"I can't say for certain, but I would assume that customers around here would be using the root symbolically in their spell-work. There are a lot of witches in town," I said, as if that much wouldn't have been immediately obvious the moment the detective set foot in town.

He ran a hand across his clean-shaven chin. "I like to think I have an open mind. Witchwood has it's fair share of strange happenings. But this is madness. This whole town seems to have gone mad." He looked up and seemed to remember who he was talking to. "Who did you sell the root to?"

"Natalia Ghoul," I promptly answered.

The detective turned his wary look on me. I probably shouldn't have sounded quite so gleeful when I said it.

"Do you have any reason to believe that the person you sold the root to might be implicated in the death of Zack Baden?" he asked.

"I'm afraid I don't know," I said, genuinely sorry. "If it helps, Natalia is a witch, and she does sell her services. There's a chance she might have met the deceased before he was, uh… deceased." I had no idea why she'd have poisoned him though.

"How about you, Ms Salem? Did you ever meet Zack Baden or his companions?"

"I didn't. Do you know anything about his companions? Their names, for example?" That was something that had bugged me ever since I'd decided to write my magazine article. No one seemed to know anything about the two companions who were supposed to have disappeared. It was like they'd never existed.

"Our investigation is ongoing. I'm not at liberty to divulge any more than that."

"No one's reported anyone missing?" I pressed, but I could read the answer from the detective's face. He was as disconcerted as I was over this missing detail.

"Are you certain you never sold mandrake root to anyone other than the person you named? Even if it was a long time ago?" He was good at avoiding questions he didn't want to answer.

"I've only ever sold some to Natalia. I had to order it in specially. I've never sold any to Bridgette Spellsworth," I added, knowing exactly what he was getting at.

He nodded. I realised he didn't look surprised. Much like me, he wasn't satisfied that Bridgette was the killer. He raised his grey gaze to meet mine and a tiny crease appeared in his forehead. "Strictly off the record… you don't seem like most of the people I've spoken to around here. How long have you lived in Wormwood?"

I wasn't foolish enough to believe that this truly was 'off the record' and not a cynical attempt to get me to open up about my own past, but I didn't mind sharing. With a bit of luck, it would help me to undo all of the dodgy things I'd done since meeting Detective Sean Admiral. "I grew up in town, but I moved away. It didn't seem like the kind of place I wanted to spend forever in."

"But you came back. Why?"

I smiled ruefully. "It's complicated. Let's just say that Wormwood is harder to leave behind than I imagined when I thought I was walking away."

The detective nodded and looked at me thoughtfully, like he finally understood something. "You just don't strike me as one of the weirdos."

I felt my eyes open wide at the sudden frankness... and at the expense of the rest of Wormwood! I found myself looking into those grey eyes, and this time, I was sure that the curiosity I saw reflected back was not due to any unanswered question.

"You've only been in a fake relationship for what, a day? And you're already thinking about cheating on your fake boyfriend?" Hemlock slipped past me leaving a strong waft of refuse in his wake. I didn't ask how he'd got out of the bin and back into the shop. Mostly because it would almost certainly make the detective retract his previous statement. And I was discovering that I liked not being one of the weirdos. It might mean I was left out of witchy affairs, but perhaps I wasn't missing out on anything good...

We both took a step closer, somehow both knowing that we were feeling the same. Was it really going to happen? After so long of being shut up in a town where no male ever noticed me, was this the golden opportunity for me to find an eligible bachelor? And a pretty darn attractive one at that...

"I can't watch. No, wait. I can," Hemlock commented from on top of a shelf. I pretended not to hear him. I was getting pretty good at doing that.

"I don't usually do this, I promise, but... would you like to go out for a drink with me sometime?" The detective kept his hands by his sides and seemed to emanate a masculine power that I was powerless to resist.

Wow. I really needed to go on more dates.

I was thinking like a Victorian nun who'd got her hands on a racy novel.

"That would be..." I started to say, but was interrupted by a sudden commotion.

"Hazel! We need you. Frogs are appearing from nowhere. I don't know what Linda did, but I hope your familiar is partial to frogs legs. We've probably got a lifetime supply for him here. At least it might save you some money on cat food," Minerva said at the same time a loud crash resounded through the house.

"I dropped the cauldron! They're everywhere. Save yourself!" Linda yelled from somewhere upstairs. "They're still multiplying!"

"Linda! I can't believe you! We're so sorry, Detective. This really is out of the ordinary for us. Usually, it's a plague of spiders," my aunt said, flicking her blonde hair over her shoulder and smiling winningly.

"Don't kiss the frogs. They don't turn into princes. I already tried that," my other aunt yelled down.

"Don't try to fob your surplus amphibians off on me! I'm still full of ritually murdered pigeon and nicely-aged fish heads. Frogs give me indigestion," Hemlock remarked from his smelly shelf.

I turned back to the detective and saw exactly what I'd dreaded seeing.

"I should check on the crime you reported when you

came in," the detective said, before hurriedly exiting the shop, giving me an alarmed backwards glance when the first of the frogs bounced into view. I didn't have to be a psychic to know what he was thinking. I was definitely back on the weirdos of Wormwood list.

I sighed and let my shoulders slump, not even caring when frogs started jumping around my ankles. My chances of finally being asked out on a date had just vanished in a puff of smoke.

Perhaps I had a magical talent after all.

6

THE SCENE OF THE CRIME

The moon was on its last night of being close to full. On the first night, a man had died in the woods. On the third, I decided it was time for me to make my pilgrimage to the cursed site.

Or perhaps I was just so desperate to escape a house full of frogs that anywhere was better than home.

Either way, I found myself walking the path that led beneath the trees and deeper into the dark forest. It was quiet tonight, apart from ominous rustling sounds and breaking twigs. Even the January wind didn't whistle through the branches, and there was the definite sense that the world was holding its breath, waiting for something to happen. In the far off distance, I could have sworn I heard a chorus of wolves howling. Hairs rose up on the back of my neck, but I ignored the strange sensation. It had to have been dogs. There were no wolves running wild in England.

My mind drifted from Hellion's threatened curse, to the tiny corpses strapped to the lampposts... and then on to the murder of the man in Wormwood Forest. His killer was still at large. It was likely that I might have missed them by moments when I'd been walking back to the shop. They might have seen me. What if they knew I was asking around about the murder? What if they were still watching me right now?

What if I'd practically done their job for them by walking into an isolated forest in the middle of the night?

I stopped and discovered I'd arrived at the edge of the clearing. The same one where it had happened. I held my breath for a moment, listening to the quiet woods with their furtive noises. Was someone lurking in the shadows? The rising hairs whispered that, yes, danger was all around. I should run, and run fast. But I knew that senses could lie - especially when you were wandering around the scene of a brutal murder on your own at the dead of night.

Police tape had been cut and lay in ribbons around the site. I wasn't the first to have come here... but the police appeared to be done with the site. At least - no one was guarding it.

I walked out into the clearing, and the hush seemed to deepen. I ignored the strangeness happening all around me, and I focused on what I was seeing, rather than what I was feeling.

There was paint on the grass. What little grass there was left, anyway. The druids and witches frequented this spot and danced circles in the clearing. I was almost surprised that the killer hadn't bumped into any of them in the midst of their murdering. I supposed the month of January was the reason why. I was already regretting wandering out into the woods wearing only a leather jacket for warmth. Dancing around sky-clad (as I'd heard witches and druids liked to) was a recipe for hypothermia at this time of year.

I knelt down and inspected the swirling paint, that had

surely been left as it had been found. My first thought was that it looked genuine. By genuine, I meant that this had been done by someone who'd copied a summoning sigil from an occult book. They hadn't just sprayed something stereotypical and had done with it. I still didn't believe that an intricately painted circle had any magical properties whatsoever, but I'd been living in Wormwood long enough to know a summoning circle when I saw one. Heck, I'd probably seen several types before I was ten-years-old, thanks to the proliferation of books on questionable magic my mother had left lying around the house. Child protection services would have had a thing or two to say about that.

I stood up and looked at the circle from a higher perspective. Then I moved my arm, mimicking the swirling motions. I wasn't exactly an expert on spray painting, but even to my untrained eye, I couldn't spot any places where the paint had coagulated, showing hesitancy. Whomever was responsible for this sigil, they'd painted it with confidence, and quite possibly, from memory.

That's probably a point against this being the work of an outsider, I silently acknowledged. My gaze travelled to the ring of trees that surrounded the clearing. There was paint on the trunks, as had been reported. This time, the cleanup crew had decided to attempt to paint over what had been there. I could follow their logic: grass grew quickly, but paint on a tree trunk could still be there in a century. And I knew there would come a time when everyone wanted to forget what had happened in this spot.

It was too bad they hadn't done a very good job. The coverup artist had used brown paint, which didn't really match the trees. They'd also made the curious error of merely painting over the marks the original vandal had created, thus forming a perfect copy of what had been there before - albeit in a slightly more camouflaged colour. In places, the brown had failed to conceal what was below, and parts of the original grey paint the killer had used showed through. I examined every symbol and was left more confused than before I'd entered the clearing. The sigil on the ground was the real deal, but the tree signs had been garish, Hollywood-style horror daubings. Why would someone who could draw a perfect sigil then splash symbols any spooky teenager would be able to pull from their brain all over the trees?

I took my phone out and snapped a picture of the seal on the ground. With a bit of luck, I'd be able to find out what it was supposed to do. The residents of Wormwood took the magical arts very seriously. This could be a major clue.

Failing that, it would be a cool picture to include on the cover of the magazine. No one would be throwing it in the recycling bin in a hurry! I'd have new advertisers signing up in no time.

I was still seeing pound signs in front of my eyes when a twig snapped like a gunshot, just beyond the ring of trees. I froze in the moonlight, knowing I probably looked like a sitting duck to anyone watching from the shadows. I'd known I was being watched. Why had I ignored it? Why had I decided to rationalise? My rebellious desire to be normal was going to get me killed after all.

The bushes opposite me started to rustle. I balled my hands into fists and willed whatever power my aunts and Hemlock seemed to believe I had to bubble up to the surface now. And then for me to equally magically know what to do with it.

I stretched my hands out in front of me and focused.

Nothing happened. No sudden burst of light and sense of power. I was just a non-magical human standing alone at the scene of murder stretching her hands out towards what could quite possibly be the killer returning to the scene of the crime.

I realised I'd shut my eyes and opened them again.

A large black kitten was sitting three-feet away from me. I jumped and nearly fell over, before my brain caught a hold of the panic I'd infused myself with.

I recognised this black cat.

"Hedge? What are you doing out here?"

Hedge blinked once by way of reply. That was his reply to pretty much everything. I often wondered if he could communicate just as well as Hemlock, but because we didn't share the familiar bond, I couldn't hear him calling out to me, and he couldn't understand what I was saying. Or perhaps he could understand, but I couldn't. Hedge moved in mysterious ways. Hemlock claimed that he could communicate with all cats, but when it came to Hedge, I didn't believe him. Especially as, according to my familiar, all he ever seemed to ask for was extra food and treats for his good buddy, Hemlock. Funny that.

In the distance, the howling started up again, followed by something that sounded suspiciously like a roar. I frowned. My dog theory didn't quite cut it when it came to roars emanating from the distant Witchwood Forest. That town had a reputation for being strange - and by Wormwood's standards, that was saying something. I'd heard from the witchy town gossip that a couple of local covens there had been wiped out under mysterious circumstances. I'd heard other things, too, but most of them had sounded like fairytales.

Until tonight... when everything suddenly seemed much, much more plausible.

"Come on, Hedge. Let's get you home," I said, as if he were the reason I'd come out into the woods in the first place. It was somehow less insane than acknowledging I'd gone sniffing around the site of a very recent murder in the middle of the night.

I felt relief wash over me when Hedge and I arrived at the first outlying buildings that signalled we were almost back in Wormwood. It was the human condition to seek safety in shelter, and I knew it was these old instincts that comforted me and whispered that I was safe now. Even if it wasn't true.

I shook the comfort of the glowing lights inside the houses away and kept my wits about me. I knew Hedge had been responsible for the rustling in the woods, but that didn't change the fact that a killer was on the loose. The pigeon and rat display showed they didn't mind making a scene, either. I didn't want to become their next grisly message.

Just as we were getting close to the high street, Hedge meowed. I immediately stopped walking and stared at him. To my knowledge, up until now, Hedge had been a mute cat.

Had I imagined him meow?

Had it been another cat?

I looked down into his mystifying yellow eyes. He blinked back at me.

I was going to walk on, but the absence of my own foot-steps allowed me to hear something else in the night.

It was the sound of laughter.

I slunk into the shadows by the side of the Post Office. Footsteps were approaching. I glanced down at Hedge, before wondering what had made me decide to hide. It was getting pretty late, but hearing someone laugh or walking about the town wasn't that suspicious. If anything, I was the sneaky one lurking in the shadows. This time, Hedge's blink seemed more deliberate. Was he telling me to stay hidden?

Had talking to Hemlock given me false expectations about the intelligence of cats?

Not that Hemlock was a genius. He just liked to think he was.

There was nothing worse for your self-confidence than losing an argument to a cat.

Whatever Hedge's blink may, or may not, have meant, we didn't have to wait long. A couple strolled into view, silhouetted against the moonlight.

"I'm not sure if I'm ready to take our plan further. You know what this town's like. People might get suspicious," a familiar female voice spoke.

"What does it matter? No one would dare to move against us... not even if they knew the truth," a man replied.

I nearly gasped out loud. His was a voice I'd already heard today.

"I don't think we can be certain of that anymore. I knew you used to worry about the Salem family, but when Freya's daughter turned out to be a dud, we all thought our troubles were over."

"She still is a dud, isn't she?" The man sounded bored by the topic.

I frowned, not liking the way I was being spoken about.

"Completely worthless," the female agreed. "Her aunts, on the other hand... They could be a problem."

"Surely they're no match for you?"

"The Salems were always a match for anyone. We've grown too used to their half-ling. They were always a threat, and they were always in charge."

"I have every faith in you," the man said, hardly able to keep the glee from his voice. He was relishing the prospect of my aunts' downfall.

"And I, you," the woman responded.

What came next was so surprising, I nearly fell out of the

shadows with shock. I'd peered around the side of the building to get a better view when the conversation had fallen silent, but the sight I'd been greeted with was truly horrible.

Hellion Grey and Natalia Ghoul were in the middle of a lengthy, passionate kiss.

7

THE GRIM

I turned my horrified wide-eyed gaze on Hedge and mouthed 'Ewww!'. He didn't respond, but I decided that his expression looked a little more distasteful than usual. Good, he agreed with me that what we'd just seen was totally gross. Totally wrong. And totally surprising.

Hellion was not what I would have called an eligible bachelor. He was short, weaselly, and made my skin crawl with revulsion. Although Natalia was probably as equally nasty as her unlikely boyfriend, I was able to grudgingly admit that she wasn't too horrible to look at. And she was probably close to a foot taller than the high magician. I knew that not all relationships had looks at their heart, but this one just struck me as strange. Might Hellion have put some kind of love spell on Natalia?

Did I even believe that love spells worked?

I pressed myself back against the wall, my head a blur of thoughts. Sometimes stressful situations could push people together to form unlikely partnerships. I ran the conversation I'd overheard through my head again. They'd been talking about taking a plan further. I'd initially assumed it was business related, but what if?

What if this plan had involved the recent murder of Zack Baden?

I might be listening to his killers talking about their plot to strike again. When I added the mandrake root I'd sold to Natalia, and Hellion's knowledge of occult symbols... it definitely painted a picture.

The stomach-churning kiss must have come to an end because a moment later I heard the footsteps continue down the street before fading away. I was left standing in the shadows feeling like someone had punched me in the gut. I'd never liked either the magician or the high priestess, but I'd still had a hard time believing that either of them would stoop so low as to actually kill someone. I'd naively believed that pain and suffering was the worst they had to hand out, but they'd graduated onto murder.

Worse still... it sounded like my aunts were their next target.

I hurried down the streets that led to home. I was still getting used to the concept of having aunts - especially aunts I suddenly lived with - but they needed to know that they were being plotted against. More than that, I was hoping they might have an idea of whether or not Hellion and Natalia were as guilty as they'd sounded.

I shook my head as I power-walked along with Hedge trotting by my side. Did I have any evidence beyond my view that the couple weren't nice people? There was the mandrake root. Beyond that, I knew it was going to be hard to forge a connection. All I could do was hope that the police investigated Natalia after my tip off and that something more concrete came up.

It was too bad. I knew in real life it was a lot harder to catch killers than it was on TV or in books. Evidence had to be solid. You couldn't throw accusations around without it. If the criminal knew what they were doing… then getting away with murder was a genuine possibility.

I walked down the empty street outside the Salem Apothecary and came to a sudden stop for what felt like the tenth time that day.

Someone had vandalised my shop.

Symbols, that were surely identical to those I'd just seen in the clearing in the woods, had been crudely painted onto the brickwork that surrounded the shop window. A headless pigeon lay on the floor on the pavement, and a red spray showed where the vandal had added a splash of colour, courtesy of the pigeon's lifeblood. The finishing touch, across the glass itself, was the large inverted pentacle and the words 'devil worshipper' painted in grey. I was willing to bet it was the same paint that had been used in the clearing.

For a moment, I just stared at it in shock… before I put two and two together. Who had I just seen walking away in the opposite direction from my shop? Which couple certainly had no love for anything Salem? I felt my fists curl into balls by my sides. If Hellion and Natalia thought they could scare me into keeping silent, they were sorely mistaken. I was going to tell the authorities everything I knew.

I unlocked the door of the shop and stepped inside. My foot came into contact with something on the floor. After my initial relief that it wasn't a frog (they'd mysteriously disappeared) I picked up the envelope I'd just trodden on, examining it with extreme suspicion.

My name was written on the front.

There was no way that I was going to open it.

I pulled my mobile phone out and called the police to report the vandalism and the suspicious activity I'd witnessed close by. Someone like Natalia would probably call me a rat, but I believed that in the eyes of the law, we were all equal. They could believe in magic all they wanted, but when it came to justice, they would get what they deserved.

At least, I hoped they would.

I was still waiting for the police to arrive when my aunts materialised in the shop.

"Where'd you go? We fixed the frog plague!" Aunt Linda announced, looking pleased with herself.

"It only took three trips to the stream at the bottom of the garden with your dustbin." Minerva shot her sister a disapproving look. "I hope you learned your lesson. What were you trying to accomplish with that spell, anyway?"

"None of your business."

"I just spent two hours chasing after frogs. You made it my business."

"I went into the woods to see the place where the man was murdered," I said.

That stopped them in their tracks.

"Ex-squeeze me?" Linda said, looking utterly gobsmacked. "You went wandering in Wormwood Forest on the night after the full moon to go and see the site of a ritual murder?"

I nodded.

She turned to Minerva. "She might be a witch after all. Did you see anything interesting? Did anything appear from the summoning seal?" she asked me.

"Linda! I'm sure she had a perfectly reasonable reason for going out there. Why did you take such a risk?" Minerva asked, far less excitably.

"I've been trying to research the murder for the lead story in my monthly local interest magazine. The magazine hasn't exactly taken off so far, and I'm hoping it will give things a boost," I explained. "I suppose I wasn't thinking about what time of day it was when I decided to go and look at the scene.

I wanted to get some photos and see if I could pick up on anything."

"Pick up on anything?" Minerva raised an eyebrow.

"Evidence. Anything that the police might have missed, or left behind. The forest is hardly an easy place to search."

For some reason, she looked disappointed.

"I didn't really think about the possibility of running into the person responsible for it all until I got to the clearing. Then Hedge spooked me." I gestured to the small black shadow, who was waiting silently by my side, watching all that was going on. It wasn't the first time that evening that I wondered what he was thinking.

"Your cat was out in the forest?" Linda queried, but was silenced by Minerva's wave of a hand. Judging by the look on Linda's face, it wasn't a silence she had much control over.

"I didn't mean the risks of running into the person responsible for that stranger's death. I meant the risks of meeting other things that walk beneath the trees when the moon is full," Minerva told me.

I waited for her to elaborate. When she didn't, I made a stab at it. "Frogs?"

"No, not frogs…" Minerva said, exasperated, before she looked past me. "Hazel, why are the police here?"

"Someone vandalised the shop. Would you mind not mentioning everything that I just told you? I know it's asking a lot, but…"

"Our lips are sealed. Salem witches stick together," Linda announced, having un-silenced herself.

"Thanks," I said, before turning to meet the police for the second time that night.

"This looks very serious. Do you have any CCTV that might

have captured the person responsible?" Detective Sean Admiral asked, looking so hopeful I immediately concluded that the police were striking out when it came to the rest of the case.

"You won't find any CCTV in Wormwood. There's some electrical interference problem that means it doesn't work here," I said. The locals liked to cite it as evidence for their magical powers, but I'd always believed the scientific explanation.

"Of course. I can't believe I forgot." The detective looked frazzled. "It's just strange in this day and age." He looked out of the window at the reverse side of the painted writing. "Were you in the shop when it happened?"

"I was out for a walk. My aunts were here, but they didn't see anything."

"We were chasing frogs," Linda unhelpfully reminded the detective.

He studiously ignored her.

"I did see Natalia Ghoul and Hellion Grey when I was out on my walk. I overheard them talking about some sort of plan they were in the middle of. I don't wish to point fingers without any evidence, but if you've spoken to Natalia about the mandrake root she purchased, might it not be plausible that she wanted to get her own back on me?"

"Hellion Grey... Why do I know that name?" the detective said.

"I mentioned him earlier. He's Wormwood's best-known practitioner of the dark arts. We're not on the best of terms either," I confessed, thinking about our earlier meeting.

"Do you think they might be involved in this act of vandalism?"

"They definitely looked like they were together." I looked out of the window and noted that one of the accompanying officers was scraping some of the grey paint off the window and into an evidence bag. I wasn't the only one who'd noticed it looked identical to the colour of paint that had been used on the trees surrounding the clearing.

"Did you find anything out when you investigated the animals that were tied to the lampposts?" I asked.

"I'm not at liberty…" the detective began but broke off with a sigh. "Nothing. No one saw anything, even though it happened in the middle of the street. If one more person suggests it was because of magic…"

I smiled ruefully. That was one of the hazards of living in Wormwood. Whenever something even slightly unusual happened, magic would be named the culprit. It was how I imagined it might have been back in time, when witches were blamed for everything from nasty falls, to milk turning sour. The only difference here was that the town celebrated anything supernatural rather than burning it.

The detective ran a hand through his dark, curling hair. "Can you think of any other reason this attack might have specifically been directed at you?"

I shook my head, before thinking about everything I'd seen that day. "It might not have a personal reason behind it at all, if it wasn't Natalia and Hellion," I reluctantly admitted. "Other businesses have been targeted as well. The lampposts… that was done right outside of the occult bookstore, owned by Mrs Spiney. I don't know if he reported it, but someone threw a rock through Hellion Grey's shop window today, along with a threatening note. Bridgette's house has also been vandalised."

"Mr Grey never reported that incident." The detective looked accusingly at me.

"I assumed he would. It was his property that was damaged and the threat was made against him." I was not going to be held responsible for Hellion Grey's decision to not involve the police.

"What a mess," the detective said, before seeming to collect himself together again. "I know it's small comfort given the damage done to your property, but I am hopeful that the culprit responsible will have made a mistake. We will do everything we can to find them. I will do everything I can," he said, turning his serious grey eyes on me.

I smiled, but it felt a little wobbly. Suddenly, a stupid piece of vandalism seemed like a really big deal. How was I going to fix up the shop with my limited funds, when the shop barely scraped together a profit each week? I would figure it out, I told myself firmly. I needed to stop being a baby.

Lights flashed in the street, and I realised people were taking pictures of the shop. A small crowd had gathered.

The detective walked outside and I followed after him, curious about the gathering audience. To my surprise, when they saw me, they shrank away. The muttering grew louder, and I was hit with disapproving looks from almost everyone present. I turned back to the window that proclaimed me as a devil worshipper, and I understood. There were some in Wormwood who resented the magical half and those who supplied it. They might not be as outspoken as the witches, healers, fortunetellers, and magicians, but they shared the town with them. It looked as if they might be thinking about taking their town back.

"Move along, please. It is late and we should all be getting home. Our investigation is ongoing and we would appreciate knowing that you are all safe in your homes," the detective said, smiling winningly at the audience.

I was relieved when they did start to drift away in dribs and drabs. There'd definitely been the feeling that something threatening had been building. "Thank you," I told the detective, trying not to wring my hands in distress, now that I looked at the damage with costs in mind.

"I'm just doing my job. Feel free to go back inside, if you would like. We'll finish our work out here, if you've shared everything you think might be useful?" He looked searchingly at me.

I looked innocently back. "I think so."

"Let me know if you think of anything else, or if anything else like this happens." He reached into his pocket and pulled out a business card.

I accepted it, knowing that earlier on this evening, it might have meant more than just business. But that was the way things happened in Wormwood. I'd already discovered that the town didn't like to relinquish its hold on those who belonged here. Was it really such a big surprise that relationships were barred by strange circumstances, too?

I left the police to it and went upstairs to bed. Hemlock was curled up on the duvet when I entered the room. Hedge had been gone when I'd returned to the shop, but that was hardly out of the ordinary. He came and went as he pleased.

"Busy evening?" Hemlock asked, rolling over and showing his fluffy belly.

I tickled it and deftly avoided the claws and teeth that tried to catch me as he curled up, like a woodlouse fleeing danger.

"It was eventful. What happened to you?" I asked and then wrinkled my nose. I'd forgotten about the promise I'd made to keep my familiar out of my room and off my bed. I began to make silent plans that involved wrapping him in the duvet and dunking him in the bath. As long as four out of his five pointy ends were covered up, I might stand a chance of walking away without needing stitches.

"I was helping out here. I supervised the frog catching."

"You mean you watched and judged."

"How dare you! I also commentated. But it's less fun

when no one can understand you." He lifted a paw to his face, the very image of a tortured artist.

"I was in the woods with Hedge looking at the murder scene."

Hemlock spat feathers out of his mouth. "What? Where was my invitation?"

"Hedge and I have a very special bond," I said, enjoying the opportunity to wind Hemlock up.

"But he's a weirdo! He's silent. He doesn't wolf his food down in one go. He's un-cat-like. It's not natural!"

"So says the talking cat," I pointed out. "Hedge meowed today."

"Hallelujah. Now tell me what you were doing out in the forest?"

"I already told you! We were looking at the murder scene."

"You mean you weren't doing any magic?" Hemlock's green eyes stared into my amber ones.

"You're jealous," I realised. "You think I ran off to do magic with Hedge."

"I am not jealous! I have my own life. I don't need you to make it interesting. If you'd asked me to go into the forest with you, I'd have said no." Hemlock lifted his leg up in the air - a sure sign he was going to attempt to end the conversation by washing his nether regions.

I grabbed the leg. "I got news for you, buddy. I'm still not magical. I can't believe I'm telling you this, but I actually tried to use magic in the clearing when something spooked me. Nothing happened. I just looked really, really stupid."

"I can't believe I missed it."

I let the leg go and smiled when it hit Hemlock in the face. "You're the worst," I affectionately told him. "You're also not staying here. You need a bath, and I need to change my covers, and quite possibly bin my entire duvet, before we can go to sleep."

"No baths for Hemlock." He primed his claws.

"Maybe not voluntarily…" I already had my hands on either side of the duvet. All I needed now was a well-executed pincer movement and Hemlock would be bath-bound.

"Hey… look at that," Hemlock said, suddenly standing and going stock still. Even though I suspected it was a stupid, childish trick, I turned to follow his gaze out of the window and across the garden.

"Nice try…" I started to say, but then I saw it.

There was a big black dog in the garden.

No. It was so large, it would probably be better described as a hound. It turned its head and looked directly up at the window, and I saw its glowing red eyes.

"What the heck is that?" I hissed at Hemlock. In my peripheral vision, I could see that my familiar had arched his back and made his fur stand on end. He was just as spooked as I was

"It's nothing good," he unnecessarily supplied.

"I should get my aunts. They seem like they would know how to deal with something like this…" I muttered, not making a move to get up from the bed. The black hound just kept on staring. Our terrible eye contact only broke when something small and black darted out across the lawn towards the beast.

"Hedge! No!" I whispered, too horrified to make a louder sound, as I watched the unmistakable shape of my second black kitten stalking across the grass towards the giant dog-thing.

"He'll be mincemeat," Hemlock said, fur still spiky.

We watched, helplessly as the cat and the hound surveyed each other, sure that Hedge was about to meet an awful end.

Then, after several tense moments, the hound trotted off towards the bottom of the garden and Hedge followed with his tail in the air.

"Plot twist! It looks like they're buddies," Hemlock said, breathing rubbish-scented breath across my face.

"What was that thing?" I muttered, still stunned by the glowing eyes. Up until tonight, if anyone had asked if I had any personal experience of the supernatural, I would have categorically told them no.

"Black shuck? Hellhound? The Grim?" Hemlock suggested, lashing his tail with excitement.

"You got that last one from *Harry Potter.*"

"I don't see you making any better suggestions."

"What was Hedge doing with it?" I wondered aloud.

"Hmm…" Hemlock said, sounding annoyingly thoughtful. "When you went out for your pleasant sightseeing stroll in the forest, did you take Hedge with you, or did you find him there?"

"I…" Hemlock already looked smug. "…I found him," I confessed.

"Judging by what we just witnessed, I'd wager you interrupted something. It does add a little pizzazz to Hedge, doesn't it? I might even consider being nicer to him, now that I know he's got a big, scary, glowing-eyed friend."

"Did you ever consider being nice for the sake of being nice?" I asked.

"Nope," Hemlock said, and tried to jump off the bed.

I caught him mid-leap in the duvet and wrapped the corners in, rolling him up, until only his head stuck out. I grinned at his glaring face. "It's bath time." I picked him up, making sure all of the pointy ends were secure and keeping the toothy one away from me.

"No! No! Noooooo!" he shouted, trying to flail around. "I

will destroy everything that you love! Your secret model unicorn collection will be history!"

I pretended I didn't know what he was talking about.

It was as I was pouring the water for the bath with Hemlock wrapped in the duvet, contemplating how I was going to make sure he got clean, whilst somehow keeping his legs from clawing me to pieces, that I reflected there was probably more reason than one that I was still single. "Do you think this is good practice for having kids one day?" I dreamily asked my furiously kicking cat, dumping him and the duvet in the water together.

"You're killing me! The water burns! It burns ussss!"

It was lukewarm and contained the extra-mild cat shampoo I'd been forced to buy from the vet when Hemlock had decided to attend his last checkup covered in fox poo. "I bet it's great practice," I said, answering my own question.

"I hate you. I wish you were dead," Hemlock said, confirming it.

8

CURSES!

"Hazel, does this envelope with your name written on the front of it belong to you?" Minerva asked when I made my appearance downstairs the next morning. I'd overslept after struggling with visions of the black dog and its glowing red eyes dancing in my head. A thousand 'what ifs' were currently hovering around in my brain.

"What envelope?" I asked, frowning and looking for some tea. Scratch that. Some coffee. Who was I kidding? Sometimes coffee was the only way.

"It was on the counter in the shop. You didn't open it, did you?" Minerva pressed.

"Of course she didn't. She'd be a cockroach, or something worse, if she had," Linda cut in.

"I meant to hand that over to the police as evidence after what happened to the shop last night. I thought it might be a threat. But I completely forgot about it…"

"It's a good thing you did forget, or that handsome police detective would be green and wart-covered right now," Linda said, smiling brightly, like this whole thing was some kind of joke. It had to be a joke, didn't it?

"Do you have any idea who might have sent you a curse? And such a mean one, too! I know they wrote your name on it, but it's completely undiscerning. The first person to pry open that flap will suffer the consequences." Minerva looked far more serious than her sister.

I walked over to the coffee tub and got out the cafetière. This conversation really needed more caffeine.

"Hellion Grey hinted... actually, he outright told me..." I amended, "...that he'd been paid to put a curse on me. He wanted me to bribe him into turning it around on my mystery enemy instead," I explained.

"That charlatan! I'm sure he would have just run back to his original customer and repeated the process," Minerva observed.

I nodded. "I came to the same conclusion. Anyway, I'm not paying anyone to put curses on anyone else!"

"Rightly so! We're here for you if you need any of that. It's what your aunts are for." Linda patted me on the arm.

"I think Hellion and Natalia might have been the ones to vandalise the shop. I told the police I saw them walking away last night, right before I came back and saw the damage."

My aunts exchanged a look. "Did it occur to you that they might have been delivering the curse?"

"I figured they'd done both. Why stop at a curse when you can also mess up someone's business?" My hand slipped. The coffee grounds spread across the counter. The morning had only just started, but I could already tell it wasn't going to be my day.

"You have to get rid of these things properly. Or they leak and spread. No one wants a leaky curse lying around the place," Linda said, regarding the envelope on the counter with distaste.

"Stop me if I'm prying too much, but why would anyone have a reason to want to curse you?" Minerva asked.

"It's her fake boyfriend. It's loooove!" Hemlock called from somewhere up above. I knew no one else could hear him, but that didn't make him any less annoying.

"I've never had a problem with Hellion before, but the Ghoul family and I…" I sucked in a breath. "…Let's just say we aren't best buddies."

"The Ghouls! I suppose some things never change," Minerva said, addressing her sister. "That was the girl we had our disagreement with, wasn't it?"

I nodded. "It's her sister who's decided she wants me cursed. I, uh, might be pretending to be involved with a man she wants for herself."

"How sordid! Is he cute? Does he have an older brother, or a lonely dad? Or even a younger brother?" Linda asked, looking immensely interested.

"Why would you be pretending to be involved with this man?" Minerva enquired, ignoring her sister.

"It's supposed to be a mutually beneficial agreement. He gets a lot of unwanted female attention. A fake relationship will hopefully stop at least some of that."

"And what do you get out of this?" Minerva queried.

"Cakes, mostly," I confessed. "Tristan is a good guy. He said he would figure something out to help me in return. At first, I think he thought the deal would be useful to me, too, because of all the men knocking down my door." I made a pointed glance towards the very empty shop doorway. "I put him right on that front. But free cake and business recommendations is pretty good, right?"

"I'm sure it is," Minerva said, doing another one of those annoying exchanges of looks with her sister. "Are you sure this man knows your relationship is genuinely fake?"

"Those were the words he used." I finally cottoned on to

what my aunts were implying. "We are friends. He started his business at the same time I took over this place. Granted, he's kind of destroying me when it comes to success… but we've always been there for each other. As friends."

"Do you like him?" Linda cocked her head and rested it on her hand, ignoring everything I'd just said.

"Just friends!" I repeated, not thrilled by the amount of attention this silly incident was garnering.

"Is he a magician?" Minerva asked, surprising me with a question I was betting might be a controversial topic.

"No, not that I know of. He moved from Brighton to Wormwood because it was the only place he could afford to rent a shop. I don't think he runs around calling himself a magician. Not that it even matters."

This time, my aunts' shared look was more of a shrug. I knew what they were thinking. It wasn't as if I was a witch anyway (according to everyone). It would hardly be a disappointment if I shacked up with a normal person.

In all honesty, if I could find a normal person to date, I would count that as a win. It was too bad the only genuinely interested party had fled when faced with an inexplicable plague of frogs. I still hadn't asked where the frogs had come from. I knew I wouldn't be given an acceptable answer.

I contemplated the envelope on the counter. *I don't believe in any of this*, I thought, daring myself to go over there and open it. My skin crawled. As much as I liked to protest that this was nonsense, and use that knowledge as a reassuring comfort blanket, there'd been things that had got under my skin recently. Things that I was still struggling to explain with my psychology and superstition theory.

Hedge slunk past me into the shop. I watched the silent cat go. He looked none the worse for his encounter with the giant black dog he'd been meeting with last night. Had I really seen those glowing red eyes? I blinked and shook my head, realising one of my aunts had said something in my direction. "Sorry?"

"I was saying that we'll take the envelope outside and properly dispose of it where it can't hurt anyone, not even the soil," Minerva explained.

"That sounds good." I was tired of protesting, especially when seeds of doubt had been planted within me.

I glanced at the clock on the wall. "I'd better open the shop. Not that anyone cares."

My aunts made noises of commiseration, which strangely did make me feel better. It was nice having family around to feel sorry for you, when you were all out of feeling sorry for yourself.

I finally managed to make my coffee and took it with me when I walked through the shop to flip the sign over and unlock the door. My aunts took the envelope with a pair of kitchen tongs (Gah! I'd picked it up with my hands!) and left in the direction of the garden. I turned back to the door, looked out... and discovered there were people standing outside.

Oh no! They must be here to trash the place. Those mutterings from last night must have turned into this, I immediately thought, my hand hesitating on the key. But then I realised I recognised the crowd. They were the supernatural community of Wormwood. And it looked like they'd all decided to visit the shop this morning.

I unlocked the door.

"Do you have any protection charms in stock? Your mother was always so good with her little bags of herbs," Agatha Frau asked, practically pushing past me to get to the stand of spell bags I'd always believed were there as tourist curiosities. "Ah, I can see she made them, but they're unactivated. That's perfect. I'll take three."

"Excuse me, do you have money bags? Freya was excellent

at money magic," the next witch said. I obligingly directed her to another dusty corner of the shop, whilst privately thinking that particular witch had to be deluded. Those charms must have sat in this shop for ever and ages... did the place look like it was rolling in money? After what had occurred the previous evening, it was pretty obvious that we were all out of protection, too. *Maybe it's because they're 'unactivated',* I thought, but it sounded so ridiculous that I nearly wanted to laugh.

Still... I obligingly stood behind the counter and sold protection charms and money bags to all who came. And then when I'd sold out of those, I went through jars of basil, allspice, angelica, cinnamon, dill, and mugwort. As the day went on, I got a glimpse behind the curtains of the supernatural community.

They were worried.

Since the murder, their revenue had dried up. Tourists, few though they were, had stopped coming to town. Worse than that, they were scared. I hadn't been the only one who'd noticed Hellion Grey's shattered window and Bridgette's boarded up house. Plus, the exterior of my shop was only too visible when they came to call. People were worried that their neighbours, who'd lived quietly by their side for years, tolerating all of the talk about magic and fortunetelling, had finally had enough. The mutterings were growing louder. It would only take one spark and the whole tinderbox would go up.

"There's a town meeting tonight in the square. I hope the mayor will be able to stop things from getting even more out of hand," a psychic told me whilst buying a lucky spell bag. We'd run out of everything else. I was so surprised by everything that had happened so far today, my mind didn't even supply a suitably witty comment about a psychic not knowing what the future held for Wormwood. Instead, all I said was 'I hope so too'.

The rush had ended when Bridgette Spellsworth slunk in.

She shut the shop door behind her and looked anxiously back out onto the street in case anyone had followed her. I waited behind the counter like a cat poised to strike. If I played my cards right, I might have just landed an interview with the prime suspect.

"How are you, Bridgette?" I asked, making sure I sounded sympathetic. Part of me crawled at what I was doing, but the other part hungered to know the truth... to find out what Bridgette knew.

"I'm not at my best, as I'm sure you can imagine," the other woman said, walking over to the counter and looking miserably at the empty racks where the spell bags had been.

"What is it you're looking for?" I asked, knowing she'd want a charm of some kind or other. "I have all of my mother's recipes. I could make you a spell bag."

Bridgette looked me up and down with the same skepticism most of the Wormwooders did. "I don't think..."

"My aunts will make it," I improvised.

"Your aunts?"

"Linda and Minerva. They're outside at the moment... dealing with something." Come to think of it, I hadn't heard from them for a while. Did it really take that long to dispose of one little envelope?

"I remember them. Salems through and through. That would be marvellous!" Bridgette's eyes lit up at the mention of the sisters. I supposed I could finally conclude that they were genuinely my aunts. Apparently, I was not a 'proper' Salem.

"Would you like some tea, Bridgette? On the house. I know you've been through a lot recently." I watched her with concerned eyes. At least she didn't see me as any kind of threat. She didn't see me as anything.

"That would be lovely," Bridgette said, walking over to the arrangement of chairs and plonking herself down.

I made the cup of tea, choosing a tea bag designed to promote honesty and truth-telling. I was hardly drugging her, but I hoped the herbs would encourage her to open up. Bridgette Spellsworth didn't believe I was capable of any real magic. I didn't believe it either, but what I did believe in was science, and science had proven that certain herbs yielded certain effects... as did the power of suggestion.

"I can't believe the police have been so focused on you. It must have been awful," I said, hoping to get the ball rolling.

Bridgette obliged. "It *is* awful. They still haven't left me alone! They don't think I'm telling them the truth." She sighed. "All I'm guilty of is looking for company. I gave that man a reading, and I liked him... so I asked him to stay. One thing led to another. Is that any great crime? When I woke up in the morning, he was gone. I assumed he'd left in the night because he didn't want to hang around for any small talk." She shrugged. "Some people are like that. I just can't believe they thought I murdered him... and then when the police let that go, they said I'd poisoned him!"

"Why would they have thought that?" I asked, although I already knew the 'poison' they were talking about.

Bridgette glanced down at the cup in her hand. "It was in the tea. I have tea that I serve to customers, you know... for readings. I don't drink it myself. That was where it was, apparently. I had no idea. I wouldn't drug my customers!"

I nodded understandingly, whilst privately thinking I could see the way the police were looking at this. They probably thought Bridgette had used mandrake root to manipulate her customers into doing things - perhaps even seeing things - to add to the experience she gave. I might have believed it myself, if I didn't know exactly who I'd sold that mandrake root to... and how difficult it was for anyone other than a business to source. There were a multitude of more suitable drugs for the job... easily purchasable, non-herbal, and without the nasty potential for accidental poisoning.

I didn't think Bridgette had poisoned that tea.

"What's your relationship like with Natalia Ghoul?" I asked.

Bridgette shot me a curious look. "You think she had something to do with all of this? I wouldn't be surprised. Nothing about that woman surprises me." Her lips thinned. "She's always been jealous, I suppose. When she was younger, she came to me for mentoring. Her mother is a fortuneteller, not a witch, and she wanted the best for her daughter. Natalia and Aurelia showed no talent when it came to precognition, but Natalia was the one who took it hardest. Before she developed her other talents, she swore that I was a fraud and that fortunetelling was mere fantasy." She snorted. "Her mother would have something to say about that! But these days, I'm not sure that even Olivia Ghoul would be willing to take on her daughter. She's gone power mad. I have a feeling that she is only going to get worse... and my feelings have a habit of turning out to be correct." Bridgette made eye contact with me.

I looked into her blue-grey irises, imagining clouds drifting there for a moment. I blinked and the image was gone.

"She's certainly ambitious," I agreed, thinking darkly of my own run-ins with the witch. Did I think she was capable of murder? Absolutely. Without a doubt. What I'd seen last night between her and Hellion had confirmed my theory that the high priestess was capable of anything. I did not believe she had any feelings for Hellion, beyond a lust for power.

Once she'd got whatever she wanted from him, he would be discarded.

"I just hope they catch whoever truly is responsible for that terrible crime. I tried to see, you know… but it's covered in mist. I can't get through it," Bridgette confessed, in a dreamy sort of way. She blinked and smiled at me. "This is good tea! I might need to order some for my own customers. Do you think we could arrange that? You should really consider giving more samples away. I know it costs money… but you know your products are good." She levelled me a sincere look.

I discovered that she was right about that. I did know that my tea was good… and it did deserve to sell.

I smiled at her - genuinely this time. "I'm sure we can arrange something, and thanks for the idea." My mind had already jumped to the bakery and the favour that Tristan owed me. What better place to test out the free sample idea? I would have to put it to him.

We both spun round when something fell to the floor and smashed.

9

STEALING THE SHOW

"Sorry! Sorry!" A mousy-haired woman popped her head out from behind one of the shelves. I hadn't even known that anyone else was in the shop. "I'll pay for that."

"It's okay. It's been there for years. I don't think anyone wanted a musical scrying bowl," I told her.

In all honesty, I was glad it was finally gone. Every now and then, even though it hadn't been wound up in forever, it would release a creepy peal of music. Horror movies eat your heart out! Having said that… the sudden musical interludes had only happened since Hemlock had arrived. He may not have opposable thumbs, but I never ceased to be amazed by the mischief he could manage with only his claws and the willpower of the devil. And they said familiars were a reflection of their witch's personality… I was skeptical.

"I'll just take some…" The witch looked wildly at the jars behind the counter. "…agrimony," she decided, before glancing sideways at Bridgette, her eyes wide. Her head snapped back forwards. "Sorry again. I didn't mean to disturb you," she muttered, as I measured out some agrimony and asked her if it was enough. She said it was fine in a vague way that made me think she hadn't come in for that at all. Once she'd paid, she dashed out of the shop and practically sprinted back down the street.

"Do you know who that was?" I asked Bridgette, confused as to why the woman had seemed so nervous. I knew there were those who still suspected Bridgette, but she was hardly going to murder anyone in broad daylight.

"Ally Paulson. Unless I'm much mistaken, she's the Wormwood Coven's newest member. Doris Donnelley retired... or was pushed out." Bridgette shrugged. "Natalia has been recruiting young blood since she took over the coven. I don't think she likes being questioned by anyone with more experience than her."

I nodded, privately thinking that Bridgette's theory seemed to check out, if this was the kind of witch she was recruiting. Ally looked too afraid to say boo to a mouse, let alone question an evil witch like Natalia.

"Thank you again for the tea. Call me when you have a protection charm ready. A money bag would be useful, too. Tell your aunts I said hello. We'll talk about the tea soon as well." Bridgette slid a holographic card across the counter towards me.

I accepted it, doing my best to not show my amusement at the highly sparkly image of Bridgette in her younger years that she'd used to advertise her business. It was clear that she was also hoping to advertise other things, too.

"Watch out for Natalia," I warned, before remembering who I was talking to.

"You're the one who needs to be careful." She looked over her glasses at me, giving me another look at those cloudy-sky eyes. "The next curse won't be so careless. They're testing your protection. You'll need all the family help you can get. Don't be too hasty in suggesting they move out."

I shifted uncomfortably, thinking about the rental property portfolios I'd gathered to give to them. They were still sitting inside a kitchen drawer... but how would Bridgette have known that? I decided to not think about it too much. Instead, I thanked her and saw her out of the shop.

I'd already decided to let my aunts stick around a little longer, hadn't I? Even though I probably couldn't afford it. *But perhaps they can pull their own weight,* I realised, thinking about Bridgette's request for spell bags. No one wanted anything I could make, but my aunts had clearly made an impact when they'd last been in town. That could work in my favour.

I considered the money I'd taken that morning. I could get used to more of that.

My aunts returned after lunchtime.

"You'll be pleased to know that the curse is gone," Minerva began.

"And we threw in a little dash of payback," Linda added, looking delighted. "But you'll have to wait and see what it is."

I didn't mind not asking. "Would you be able to make some protection charms and money bags for the shop? I sold out this morning. No one wants them if I make them." That still peeved me.

Minerva walked over and rested a hand on my shoulder. "It will be the least we can do. The people living here are worried, aren't they?"

I nodded. "I still don't understand..." I began, but trailed off. Was I really about to whine to my aunts about not having a gift I didn't even believe existed? I bit my lip and found a different question rising inside of me - one that had been growing ever since they'd arrived on my doorstep.

"Why are you really here?" I asked them. At first, I'd assumed that they'd needed a place to stay. Perhaps their lives had turned out even worse than mine. I'd been okay with the idea of offering sanctuary, but I didn't think that was it. In spite of all the crazy that had happened since my aunts had come to stay, I knew they could take care of themselves. Which begged the question... why were they really here?

"We are here for you. We lost a sister, but you lost a mother. You need your family." Minerva slid into a chair beside me.

I looked at her. Even though I wasn't psychic, I could tell there was something else. Something I wasn't being told. "What is it?" I asked, knowing she would understand.

"This is an important time of your life. At least... we think it is." Linda glanced up at Hemlock, who blinked his green eyes at her.

"Don't look at me. I don't think you're special at all," Hemlock chimed in.

I glared at him.

"You really think I might have some magical talent that's about to wake up in me?"

My aunts exchanged a glance. I wished they'd stop doing that.

"It's a little more complicated than that," Minerva said.

"Or at least... it might be," Linda added.

"I just want to know," I said, fed up with secrets and half-truths.

"And you deserve to. We should talk more about it tonight... a good long talk. For now, I think you have business to attend to and probably more charm preorders to take. We'll get started on a batch right away, won't we Linda?"

"Ohhh, but I was going to spend the afternoon trying to make George Clooney fall in love with me."

"Linda! You know that is misuse of magic. You got caught last time. Do you really want to go back to that witch detention centre?"

"Maybe. The guard was kind of cute. I think I made a great impression. Anyway... that was when there was still a Witch Council." She grinned.

"You're a hopeless case," Minerva decreed, before looking past me and nodding with her head.

I followed her gaze. The rush was back. It would appear that Wormwood had been on lunch break, but now the surprising number of customers were continuing to flock in. I needed to make a 'preorders available' sign - and fast.

I jumped to it and lost myself in the whirl of business, taking orders left, right, and centre. I even forgot all about the conversation my aunts had promised to have with me that evening.

———

Half the town took to the streets that evening.

I remembered the mention of a town meeting being held in the square, but I also sensed that people were here for another reason. Bad things had been showing up in town. Nasty signs that no one wanted on their front doorstep. I could feel the tension in the air. The residents wanted to find the person responsible for everything that had turned their town sour.

I wouldn't want to be that person, if the mob caught them.

"I suppose we'll have to talk secrets after the meeting," I said to my aunts when we left the shop.

I locked the door behind me and wondered about the wisdom of leaving at all. I knew it was nonsensical. The shop had already been vandalised. What more could anyone do to it? I'd been too busy with customers to repaint today. My aunts had cleaned the blood from the window, but that had been the grand total of the clean-up operation. Secretly, I was in no big hurry to remove the graffiti. I didn't have much in the way of marketing campaigns, and pity was as good at making sales as anything.

"Where does the mayor stand on all of this?" Minerva asked as we followed the crowd of people towards the square.

"I suppose we'll find out," I answered.

"She means: is he one of us, or one of them?" Linda elaborated.

I looked at my aunts. "Is that really the way it is? Us and them?"

"Trust me. That's the way it'll feel when they break out the flaming torches and pitchforks. Look." Linda nodded her head towards a tarot reader's tiny shop. We watched as one of the many people on the street that night spat on the window in clear disgust.

"Not everyone feels that way. There are always extremes in any community." I wasn't willing to believe the worst in everyone, based on the actions of a few.

"We'll see. I just hope both factions are equally repre- sented tonight... or things could go medieval real fast," Linda said, casting looks around.

We walked into the square and waited for something to happen. Behind us, a scuffle broke out, but it was swiftly broken up by those surrounding the men who'd decided to fight. I didn't recognise either of them, but it hardly helped the mood. The crowd was shifting suspiciously, and everyone was watching everyone else. We all knew that the town was likely harbouring a murderer - potentially a serial killer - and it could be any one of us.

"Good evening everyone! I am your mayor, Gareth Starbright. First of all, may I say what a great pleasure it is to see so many of you here tonight. I know it's cold, which is why I'm going to make this brief, so you can be home and warm again soon." He paused to smile. "I am sorry that it is under this grave set of circumstances that our town has needed to come together, but tonight, we hope to allay fears and assure everyone that everything is being done within our power to stop the blight that is upon us. Detective Admiral has agreed to speak to us all today in order to give an update on the police investigation into the tragedy that occurred in Wormwood Forest." The mayor stepped aside from the podium that had been set up for the meeting and allowed the detective to take his place.

"The mayor is dreamy! I remember his father being cute... but the son is a definite improvement."

"Linda! Do you ever think of anything else? Don't be so superficial. That man up there has a challenging job to do," Minerva chided.

Linda turned to me. "Is he single?"

"You're too old for him. Or anyone around here!" her sister interrupted.

"When are you going to let me have some fun?"

"When you start acting your age!"

"Shhh!" I said, desperate to hear what the detective had to say. This whole crowd felt like it was balancing on a knife edge.

"...making advances in our investigation, but there are still questions that need to be answered. We value your constant vigilance and welcome any witnesses who might have seen the perpetrators of the recent vandalism, which may be connected to the case," the detective was saying.

"Vandalism? It was mutilation! How long before they kill again? It's obvious it's just a matter of time..."

*"Where are the police? I don't see any of you around town until **after** a crime has been committed. You're supposed to protect us, but you don't care!"*

"We all know what the problem is. WHO the problem is..."

I looked around with growing anxiety as the shouts escalated. I knew what was coming next, but it was still a shock when it did.

"It's the witches. They did this. This is our town. We should take it back!"

"We need to work together in order to solve this crime," the detective called over the growing hubbub. But his words weren't heeded. People started to push and panic, as everyone felt the enemy was among them - one side or the other. My aunts had been right to believe there were sides. We'd just reached the boiling point.

"STOP!" a commanding voice covered the square. To my intense surprise, everyone did as it commanded. They froze and looked towards the owner of the voice. "There is no need for unrest. I have travelled here to help you. Your police may be ill-equipped, ill-experienced... but these cases are my bread and butter. I give you my word, I will solve this case, I will catch the person responsible, and I will protect all of you."

The crowd parted before the owner of the voice when he walked through them to approach the podium.

"And who are you?" Detective Admiral asked over the microphone.

"You can call me Detective Heathen. Jesse, to my friends. The mayor invited me here to..." He seemed to consider for a moment. "...assist in these troubling times." The stranger smiled around and I felt something pass through the crowd.

A thrill, and something else. Did I sense that they liked this man?

He stepped up on the podium next to the police detective, and I finally got a good look at him. He was slightly shorter than the other man, but his shoulders were broader and he had the look of a man who knew how to fight dirty... and win. His dark hair was cut in a fashionable short-sided style, without being ridiculous. This new detective dressed smartly, in black, but not pretentiously. I saw the glint of silver around his neck, but couldn't tell what pendant he wore. Lastly, there were his eyes.

They were amber, just like mine.

"Are you a member of the police force? I have jurisdiction in this town," Detective Admiral said, grabbing the microphone and moving away from the stranger.

"Detective Admiral. We're just trying to help..." the mayor tried to jump in, but was ignored by the policeman.

The stranger didn't seem bothered, and his voice had a way of carrying un-amplified... almost as if by magic. "I am not affiliated with the law in any way, but I still practice justice. That is the only law that matters."

"Here, here!" someone called. The stranger smiled.

"This is a police matter. If you interfere with our investigation, you will face the full weight of the law. The real law!" The detective was losing the crowd and he knew it, but there was nothing he could say or do to match this avenging angel, who had just strolled into town and captivated everyone with his charisma.

"What *is* he?" I whispered to my aunts before realising what I'd just said.

"I have no idea," Minerva answered.

"But I want some of it," Linda added.

I looked back to the front of the crowd, as Detective Admiral tried to order everyone to disperse.

"Go in peace. I take full responsibility for this town... and I'm going to be around for a while," the stranger said. It was after his words that people began to drift away, and the tense mood evaporated. Instead, there was a kind of excitement in the air, like the night before Christmas. Things were going to get better, and more than that, something special was going to happen. The feeling was so strong, it felt like it was practically forcing itself down my throat.

I stayed in place longer than the rest of the audience, trying to understand what I was feeling. When my thoughts cleared, I discovered I was looking towards where the stranger stood next to the podium... and he was looking right back at me.

My stomach seemed to flip under his attention, and I felt the rush of blood surge towards my face. All of these things I discovered I was able to examine in a detached manner - just as I was able to examine the stranger. His mouth quirked up at one side and those amber eyes seemed to burn brighter than was natural. Stranger still, I thought mine might be glowing in return.

The stranger winked at me, and I felt my limbs turn to jelly. All of a sudden, I couldn't remain outside of myself any longer. Feelings that I'd never felt before spiralled up through me, power, lust, and love, mingled into one. This was more than just a crush on the new man in town.

I dug my nails into my hand, feeling the pain. For a moment, my head cleared. I was free from this strange trance. Without another second's thought, I turned my back on 'Detective Heathen' and walked out of the square and into the icy embrace of the winter's night.

Did that really happen? I wondered, as I walked through the emptying streets.

I didn't know for sure. I felt like I didn't know anything anymore.

JESSE'S GIRLS

I sobered up the next day.

The return of my senses was largely helped by the fresh influx of customers, all buying herbs I knew could be used in love spells. I wasn't the only one who'd been caught under the stranger's influence. Now that I had space and time to think about it, I realised it was hardly surprising. With so few new faces in town, a stranger - and a handsome one at that - was bound to generate his fair share of interest. I would not be joining the queue of women throwing themselves at him.

Or rather - trying to bewitch him into throwing himself at them.

These were dangerous times for the new detective in town.

What makes him a detective, anyway? I wondered when the crowds died down around lunchtime. Detective Admiral certainly hadn't been impressed. I could only assume he'd given himself that title because he was a private investigator, but weren't they usually employed by someone? I knew the stranger had implied that the mayor had asked him to come, but it felt strange that the normally pragmatic mayor would risk alienating the police by calling in a stranger to do their job for them…

The stranger's presence here was a mystery, as was the man himself.

"Hemlock… have you heard anything new today?" I asked my familiar.

The big kitten stretched himself out in a patch of sunlight on the counter. "Nothing beyond talk about how darned attractive this new guy in town is. Even the men are taken with him. Is he smuggling catnip in his shorts?"

"That is a good question," I replied, not thinking about catnip… but something else. If what Hemlock was reporting was true, it would appear that there was no one in town who didn't love 'Detective Heathen'. I knew it was cynical, but in my experience, there was such a thing as *too* perfect. He was hiding something.

"I hope you've got your love spell ready…" Hemlock said. He disappeared beneath the counter, chortling to himself.

I looked up and realised what he was talking about. The stranger had just walked into the shop.

"How can I help you?" I asked, determined not to give him any kind of special treatment. I did not know this man, and I was not going to fall for his charms, either.

We made eye contact and his amber eyes seemed to flare, the same way they had done the previous evening. I put it down to the sunshine's reflection.

"You're Hazel Salem, aren't you? I was told you'd know the answer to a question I have," he said, approaching the counter without looking at anything in the shop… apart from me.

If he kept this up, I was probably going to do something stupid… like forget how to breathe. "That would depend what your question is."

"Mandrake root. I'm on the hunt for the person you sold it to."

"She's probably on the hunt for you, too," I said, before clamping my hands over my mouth. How had that slipped out? It felt like I hadn't had an influence over my thoughts translating into actual words.

The stranger looked amused. "And she would be?"

"Natalia Ghoul. Good luck, Detective," I added.

"Thank you. And call me Jesse." His eyes found mine again in a moment that felt like it spanned the entirety of time as we know it.

"I don't smell any catnip, but there is *something* about him," Hemlock said to me, jumping up on the counter and inspecting our visitor.

Jesse glanced down at him.

"Don't take this the wrong way... but he's out of your league. You should definitely consider a love spell," my familiar added.

I shot daggers at Hemlock, but refrained from pushing him off the counter. Even though he really deserved it. Weren't familiars supposed to bolster your confidence, not strip it away with cruel statements of realism?

I smiled what I hoped was a vague farewell at the new guy in town, but was surprised to see a flash of amusement dance across his features - almost as if he'd understood everything that Hemlock had just said. But that was impossible... wasn't it?

I started to ask, but stopped myself. I'd already said something I regretted in this conversation. I wasn't going to make things worse by asking if he could hear my cat talking.

"Bye, Hazel. I'll be seeing you around," Jesse said, inclining his head and smiling a slanting smile that made me feel like he was seeing everything that I was, and I couldn't move under his gaze.

"See you soon," I squeaked out, right before he shut the shop door behind him.

I stood in silence for several moments after he'd gone, feeling the air move around me and letting it take the remainder of his subtle leather and smoke scent away. I wanted to avoid inhaling it, as if it were some kind of dangerous drug. *Who **is** he?* I wondered.

"There's definitely *something* about him," Hemlock repeated. "I don't like it."

I knew exactly what he meant.

Any normal person might have appreciated the silver lining of all the fresh business the disaster and the stranger had brought my way. But instead of stopping to smell the roses, I found myself drawn deeper into the mystery that no one could solve, and the killer no one could find. I was supposed to be researching an article, but the more I found out, the more questions I had... and one of these questions kept coming back.

Who was Zack Baden?

The papers had claimed he'd been identified by ID left on his corpse, and he'd also given his real name to Bridgette. Beyond that, no one had come forward to claim him. No friends or family. And yet... he'd come to town with two other strangers.

It didn't add up.

The first place I searched was online. Sure, it was a simple approach, and I had no doubt that the police would have looked there first, but a lot of people posted a lot of information without a second thought of who might be viewing it.

I started with Facebook. Zack Baden was easy to find. I recognised his profile picture as the one the newspaper and the police had used when they'd been looking for witnesses. He had friends, but the evidence would suggest that they weren't real ones - the kind who would actually help you out if you were in a bad situation, or... you know... dead.

Even though I knew the police must have done all this and found nothing of value, I searched through his pictures, hoping to find something useful. There were a few shots of him with other people, but they were years old and nothing jumped out at me.

His newer shots were all selfies, apparently taken for self-enjoyment, because no one had liked them. I found myself looking at a male-model type shot featuring a t-shirt that a male-model type man could have worn and got away with. *A man like Jesse Heathen*, I thought before silencing my runaway mind. Unfortunately, Zack Baden hadn't been one of those men. There wasn't anything particularly wrong with him, apart from a cruel look in his eyes and an ugliness of the face that was nothing to do with genetics. It was his character on display.

"So, he wasn't likeable... that doesn't mean he should be dead," I muttered, reminding myself of what was important.

My eyes drifted down the picture, from the gold medallion he wore, to the try-hard cowboy boots.

I came back to the medallion... enlarging the picture as much as Facebook would allow. "Huh!" I said, when I was just about able to pick out the design. It was a circle made up of arrows, all pointing outwards. It wasn't a symbol that most people would have imagined was anything other than a pretty design, but any Wormwooder would have recognised it. There were many fans of Aleister Crowley in town. This was a symbol of chaos magic. *Zack Baden was interested in the dark arts,* I concluded. It shouldn't have come as much of a surprise. After all, he'd chosen to visit Wormwood. Not many normal people did that.

On a strange whim, I went back over to google and searched for: 'summonexcalibur Chaos' - Zack's url tag on Facebook, and the symbol on his necklace.

I wasn't disappointed.

A blog page titled 'Summon Excalibur - the diary of a Chaos Magician' popped up. *If the police have found this, they've been keeping it quiet,* I thought, feeling a thrill at potentially having uncovered something that no one else had yet seen. I had made a breakthrough.

I clicked on the site and began trawling through many cringeworthy accounts of tried and failed rituals and strange ideas that made no sense when you gave them even a moment's scrutiny. I was about to give up when I saw something else in a photograph. It was an image of Zack's altar - that looked more like a collection of sparkly and evil looking items that I recognised as tourist tat, than anything functional.

But it wasn't the altar that drew my attention. It was the business card at the edge of the shot with the signature scrawled across the picture, like a celebrity signing their autograph.

Hellion Grey - A Nasty Piece of Work!

Now I could be certain that I'd seen something the police had missed. Otherwise, Hellion Grey would be down at the station in handcuffs right now. Zack Baden was supposed to be a stranger to Wormwood, but I was looking at a piece of evidence that hinted strongly otherwise. He'd known Hellion Grey... and in Hellion Grey's own words: He was a nasty piece of work.

I probably should have told the police what I knew. That would have been the sensible thing to do... the adult thing to do. But I had a score to settle with Wormwood's most hellish couple, and before I could consider the consequences of potentially confronting a killer, I was on my way to the Ghoul residence.

I wasn't sure why that was the first place I decided to look - call it intuition - but when I turned onto the street I knew. I just knew that they would both be there. "Round two," I muttered to myself, remembering the first time I'd visited the Ghoul residence. I'd been invited to a coven meeting, but like the prom queen voted in to make a fool of her, it had been a cruel trick that I'd only narrowly escaped. This time, I wasn't going to give any of them the chance. I was going to find out the truth, and then I was...

What was I going to do?

I hesitated in the road outside the house as common sense finally flooded back in. How had I made it so far without stopping to think that far ahead? I took a faltering step backwards and someone grabbed me.

11

CONFESSIONS OF A CROOKED COVEN

"**S**top fighting!" a voice hissed.

I was surprised to find myself obeying it.

I turned my head and recognised the man who'd just yanked me into the alley by the Ghoul residence. "I should have guessed it was you," I said, still wondering how it was that Jesse Heathen had the power to tell me and everyone else in town what to do.

"Good to bump into you again, too. Now what in the dark place's name are you doing walking towards here like you're on a warpath?" he asked.

I looked into his face and discovered something interesting.

"You already know the answer. You're here because you think they did it, too."

For just a second, Jesse looked mightily peeved. "Sure. But notice how I'm not rushing in like a bull in a china shop? These are dangerous people. You've lived in this town for a lot longer than I have. Why don't you realise that yet?"

"They just think they're scary," I protested, but the waver in my voice hinted that I didn't really believe all of this was completely pretend. Not anymore. Not after everything that suddenly seemed to be crawling through the cracks in the fence I'd built around my mind.

"Very convincing." Jesse considered me for a long moment. "I can see that we're both on the same trail. But I'm not sure why you're even looking. It doesn't matter," he said, waving a hand to stop me from cutting him off. "I want to propose a truce. You tell me what you know about this power couple and I'll tell you what I've found out."

I stayed silent for a moment, wondering why I was the one who had to go first, before I decided it was ridiculous to keep quiet. Hadn't I been about to bottle it and go running to the police? Telling Jesse Heathen probably wouldn't do any harm, and if he was true to his word, I might learn something new in return.

"I saw Hellion's business card in a photo on a blog that belonged to the murder victim, Zack Baden. Zack seemed to believe he was a magician. I think he probably knew Hellion… which he, in turn, lied about. No one was supposed to have known Zack before he turned up dead."

"Great. That's the same thing I found," Jesse said, nodding along to my words.

I glared at him.

His mouth quirked up on one side. "Fine. After you told me that Natalia was the one who bought the mandrake root, I did some more digging. It turns out she had dealings with Zack Baden before he came to town and got himself murdered. She has a high-end spell business that she runs online. It's successful enough that I was able to access her yearly accounts. Then, it was a simple matter to contact her accountant and persuade her to share a little more exclusive information."

"Her?" I frowned.

"She doesn't use Gareth Starbright for her business

accounts. I don't think Natalia wants it put about town how, exactly, she makes her money. And any fool would be able to figure that much out."

"I thought you said she sells high-end spells?"

Jesse raised his eyebrows and waited for his implied meaning to sink in. *Oh.* He meant that her spells came with some added extras thrown in. Ick. I guess it explained how the sisters were able to afford such a big house.

"A chat with Ms Ghoul's accountant revealed that - like any business owner - she had trouble with a few customers who didn't want to cough up cash. Guess who's name was on the 'Unpaid Invoice' list?"

"Zack Baden," I filled in, as I knew I was supposed to.

"You get a gold star!" Jesse said, before grinning. "Maybe I should keep you around as a sidekick. It's fun being patted on the back."

"Sidekick?!"

"Mentee?" Jesse suggested.

I crossed my arms.

He carried on grinning. "Anyway… I applied some pressure to the accountant, and it turns out that Natalia has some pretty novel ways of extracting cash from customers who don't pay their bills. Namely, she sets her attack dog on them… which brings me on to…"

"…Hellion Grey," I finished, and then glared at Jesse Heathen's smug face. I was no one's sidekick!

"I wonder when their business arrangement turned personal," I mused, and had the satisfaction of seeing surprise flash across Jesse's face. Even the hotshot new detective in town wasn't infallible.

"What do you say we go and ruffle a few feathers?" he asked. For a second, I could have sworn his eyes glowed again.

"Lead the way." I may have been about to march into the

lion's den a few moment's prior to being dragged away by the detective, but now I'd cooled down somewhat, I knew it would be a mistake to rush in there on my own.

Jesse had just revealed that Natalia used some pretty questionable methods to push people into paying outstanding balances, and there was still the question of her having potentially supplied the mandrake that poisoned Zack Baden, before murdering him in the forest. There was only one thing I thought Natalia loved more than money and sneering at people... and that was power.

There was something about Jesse Heathen that made me think he could handle this pair. I thought he had a power of his own. I just didn't yet understand it.

"Let's see what's behind door number one," Jesse said, knocking on the door and flashing me a beautiful smile. Perhaps it would be worth being his sidekick just for that...

I really needed to snap out of it.

"Yes?" Natalia purred, opening the door and seeing the detective standing there.

Her smile faded when she saw me. "What do **you** want? I thought it was already abundantly clear that you don't fit in with us." Natalia made it obvious that she was including the detective in her neat little club that I wasn't a part of.

"And I'm glad of it. My aunts send their regards," I tacked on, knowing it was the best dig I could make. Part of me wanted my aunts to be right about this whole magical late developer thing. If I were to suddenly come into some magnificent magical powers, that would certainly show Natalia!

It was no wonder why nothing had manifested. I still had the mind of a secondary school kid.

"I was wondering if we might trouble you for some of your time? Hazel is helping me with a few of the case details, but I think you might be able to assist me in the investigation," Jesse said, smiling widely at Natalia, smooth as melted chocolate.

I resisted the urge to kick him. He'd just made me sound like his PA!

"Is the shop and that rag you call a magazine not making ends meet? How terrible. I would *never* have guessed that might be the case..." the detestable Natalia said, delighting in the idea that I might have been forced to take on another job.

I opened my mouth to spit out the little piece of information about the exact nature of Natalia's own business I'd just learned, but Jesse turned and gave me a look of warning so strong that I shut it again. Oh, right. I should be thinking about the case.

"Is Hellion Grey here?" the detective asked, making his question as casual as possible.

"Yes. You came at exactly the right time. We're having a coven meeting, but I'm sure we can both spare a few moments to answer your questions, Detective."

Jesse reached out and took her hand. "I can't thank you enough for your help in this matter."

Natalia was practically glowing with joy. I silently wondered what Hellion would make of the way his new beau didn't seem all that committed to him.

"Does she have to come?" Natalia whined, not even looking my way.

"Yes. She's taking notes," Jesse explained.

I reluctantly pulled out the notepad and pen I carried with me everywhere - just in case a good news story came my way. Jesse slipped me a wink when Natalia had turned around. I wondered how he'd known about the notepad, or had he just guessed? It was another thing to add to the infuriating mystery that was Jesse Heathen.

I was surprised to hear raised voices when we crossed the threshold of the Ghoul residence.

"Give me a second," Natalia said, flashing a smile at Jesse, but looking harassed.

The detective raised an eyebrow at me. We followed behind, peering past when she walked into the living room.

Hellion was standing at the front of the group of witches with his hands raised to subdue the protests directed his way. Judging by the expressions on the rest of the coven members' faces, they weren't enjoying whatever sermon he'd been preaching.

"Ladies… this is the best decision for everyone. Joining forces equals a stronger, better coven. Your high priestess agrees! That is why we stand together, united," he said, turning and smiling a sickly smile when Natalia reentered the room. It slipped when he saw the detective standing there. I'd have liked to think that Hellion had realised he was in some kind of trouble and was smart enough to be concerned, but I thought it had more to do with the arrival of a young and attractive male competitor.

"What is this? Are you joining us, Detective?" Hellion said, raising his voice and shooting us a sardonic smile.

Yup. This was definitely about being the dominant male.

"We are only a humble coven, but I'm sure we'd be delighted to add your presence to our meeting. Do you dabble in the dark arts?" Hellion's maggot-eating grin was a sure sign that he was trying to scare the detective.

"I do not dabble," Jesse said, looking utterly bored by this odd display. "I am here to ask some questions. Perhaps your friends might even be able to help."

That was upping the ante. With the unrest so painfully obvious in the coven right now, question time had just turned into trial by jury.

Jesse Heathen strode out into the middle of the room and every single witch present snapped to attention. Hellion Grey didn't stand a chance.

"I'm going to start by asking if anyone here knows anything about how dried mandrake root ended up in Bridgette Spellsworth's teabags?" Jesse said, surprising me. Weren't we here to extract a confession of murder, not mess around with teabag poisoning?

There were snickers, but no one answered.

Jesse nodded, like he'd been expecting as much. "Natalia… I know you bought the root. Why did you poison the teabags? One theory I have is that you knew Bridgette served the tea to her customers. Once one of them had got a good strong dose, they would be easy to lead into the forest and kill - to fuel a ritual you believed would grant you greater powers."

Natalia's mouth dropped open. She looked at Jesse like she didn't know if he was being serious or not. "I never did any of that! I bought the mandrake, but it was for something else. I've already explained all of this to the police."

"What was it for?" I jumped in, unimpressed by this excuse.

Natalia glared at me. "A private condition! Never you mind. I explained it to the police. If it was good enough for them, it's good enough for you, half-witch."

I felt the sting of the insult, even though I'd never worried about my 'purebred' magical heritage. Plus, no one, including me, knew who my father was. He could have been anyone. For the briefest of moments, I wanted to tell Natalia something about her own father. If anyone was a half-witch here, it was her. But I reminded myself that I'd made a deal regarding that matter. And even though it would feel good for a second, part of me delighted in keeping that dark secret from Natalia, and knowing a truth she would never guess.

"Stop this! Stop it! She's covering for me."

Everyone turned and stared at the mousey witch who'd spoken and looked terrified by her own words. I recognised her as Ally Paulson, the witch who'd come into my shop the other day, before practically running out again when she'd seen Bridgette.

Oh.

I thought I was starting to understand why.

"Ally!" Natalia looked furious.

"It was me," Ally said, stepping forwards and looking towards the detective. "I'm the one who poisoned the tea. I did it to ruin Bridgette's business... not because I wanted to kill anyone. I would never, ever kill anyone!" Her bottom lip wobbled.

"What did you have against Bridgette?" Jesse asked, his voice kinder than I'd heard it before.

"She stole my husband. I know he was a lousy cheating good-for-nothing. I'm not arguing that, but she didn't need to take him. She could have had anyone else! But she carried on with him, right under my nose." Ally looked devastated. "I told Natalia about what happened. She suggested I get revenge, but I was the one who did it, not her. She got me the mandrake root and kept Bridgette busy, whilst I added it to the loose tea leaf jar she serves to her customers. It felt great for a while! I wanted her to get a taste of her own medicine. I wanted her to know what it felt like having your life ruined. But then... but then..."

"Someone got murdered," Jesse finished, when Ally seemed unable to.

"I never meant for that to happen. I didn't do it. I swear! I'll come clean to the police about the mandrake. I know I should be punished for that. I was just too scared before, and Natalia said everything would be all right." Ally smiled at the high priestess. "I'm sorry. You've done so much for me."

"That's quite all right," Natalia said, looking as gracious as I'd ever seen.

I didn't buy the act for a second. Natalia was playing it up for the cameras - or in this case, for Jesse Heathen. I really hoped he wasn't buying her 'holier than thou' act. I'd heard from Bridgette herself that she and Natalia were hardly best buddies. I doubted she would have lifted a finger if attacking Bridgette hadn't also benefited her. I was also skeptical that Ally was the one who'd come up with the plan. That kind of evil endeavour had Natalia written all over it.

"I'm glad we've solved that mystery. Thank you for your honesty, Ally," Jesse said, giving her a grateful smile that made her blush to her roots. "I have one more question, and then I won't take up any more of your valuable time."

"Hear, hear," Hellion muttered, very audibly.

Natalia shot him a disgusted look. Their relationship was *clearly* going well.

"Mr Grey, what kind of curse or hex did you sell to the murder victim?"

Hellion's expression turned ashen. "I didn't sell him any curse or hex."

"Then what did you sell him? I doubt a man like you gives freebies away."

He has that right, I thought, remembering back to Hellion's attempted extortion.

"I don't recall selling him anything. I never met the man!" the magician protested, looking even shadier than usual.

The detective shot him a look that said he saw straight through the act. "I have some pretty compelling evidence that you did. I'd be happy to share it with you... or you could save me the trouble and think again. I'm sure a man like you sells to so many people, it's hard to remember every face."

For a moment, the two men stared one another down. I kept my eyes fixed on the ground, wondering what would happen if Hellion asked for the evidence. All I had was a photo posted by the dead man, which contained a signed business card that he plausibly could have obtained from anywhere. I believed Hellion, conceited as he was, had personally signed it, but there was no real proof.

Hellion broke first. "I suppose I might have sold him something. It's just as you said… I sell a lot of things to a lot of people, and I try not to remember their names and faces. In my line of work, it's better not to know more often than not." He grinned in a predatory manner that made my skin crawl.

"Is there a chance that this man didn't pay you? He had a history of doing that," Jesse said, glancing across at Natalia when he said it. The flash of panic in her eyes was more than enough confirmation that her accountant had been telling the truth. She'd known Zack Baden, too.

"No. I ask for cash up front," the magician said, as if this proved he was no fool.

I can't imagine why, I thought, considering the dubious claims Hellion made, and the even more dubious customers he dealt with.

Jesse nodded. "But you help other business owners out when they have problems getting what they're due." It wasn't a question.

Natalia looked as stiff as a board. Even Hellion was rattled.

The magician licked his lips. "You want to be careful what you're saying, boy. You don't know who you're messing with."

"A couple of murderers?" Jesse merely looked curious when he asked it.

"I am not a killer! He might be. But I am not," Natalia protested, physically taking a step away from her new boyfriend.

"I have never killed anyone. I've sold curses that will do the job… but never personally… I would never…"

"Botch a blood sacrifice by throwing together a mixture

of genuine occult symbols, the summoning sigil of the demon Abyss, and a few horror movie knock-offs for good measure?"

The room fell icy silent. Everyone stared at the detective.

He smiled a grim smile. "I've done my research."

"I am innocent. However, if I may prey upon your patience for just a little longer, witches have been historically known to desire demons. Cavorting with them is practically in their spell book!"

"How dare you! You're the one who boasts about summoning spirits and demons as part of your unique selling points. You're a snake and a fraud!" Natalia bit back.

The detective watched the back and forth with a twinkle of amusement in his eyes. When the argument simmered down to a venomous staring match, he made a noise of amusement. "Thank you for your assistance. We shall leave you to your gathering." He turned and beckoned me to follow him.

I glared at him for having the nerve to treat me like a servant, but there was no way I wanted to stick around in this toxic environment.

I waited until we were outside and had rounded the corner of the street before I reached out and grabbed his arm. "What are you doing? I thought you were about to get a confession out of them. They practically admitted it!"

Jesse looked amused. "Do you really believe they did it? Think about it."

I frowned. "Maybe. They both had a problem with the murder victim, and they both didn't admit they knew him. Probably because they had something to hide - something like murder. Plus, they're the only people I've found with a prior connection to the dead man."

Jesse turned away from me and laughed. "You do know it's far more likely that the killer is someone the dead man knew well- who probably also knew that killing him in this way, and in this town, would point fingers at particular people? Consider this - if you were that pair, and you really wanted to kill a man for your own evil ends, would you firstly, do it so obviously, and secondly, make a confusingly bad mess of it?!"

"They're hardly a great team," I pointed out. "You ripped them to shreds in seconds."

The detective turned back around and nodded. "I did. It was even easier than I'd imagined."

"Was that the whole purpose? To put the cat amongst some very dim pigeons?"

"I wanted to make sure I was correct before going after the real culprit. It's important to eliminate every possibility, no matter how ridiculous you might imagine it to be." He turned his head to look at me. "Couldn't you see it when we were in there? You were born in this town. I've heard things about your family."

"See what?" I asked, mystified.

Jesse looked deep into my eyes, his amber orbs reflecting my own. He held my gaze for what felt like a minute, inspecting everything he saw there. "Never mind," he said, before walking off down the street without so much as a good bye.

Whatever he'd been looking for, it was obvious that he hadn't found it.

12

THE GREATER GOOD

I decided to take a break from the biggest story in Wormwood. After the events of the morning, I felt sick of the entire thing. I wasn't going to throw in the towel on my piece of investigative journalism, but I definitely needed to switch my focus for a bit. Especially where Jesse Heathen was involved. For a while, I'd toyed with the idea of investigating him. Who was he? Why had the mayor invited him to come to town? I had so many questions, but some inner intuition told me I would find nothing, no matter how hard I looked. There was *something* about Jesse Heathen. I felt, deep in my bones, that I would get to the bottom of it one day… but today was not going to be that day.

Instead, I investigated my aunts.

Linda and Minerva Salem were surprisingly simple to find online. They didn't go in for any of the modern social media or blogs, but if you knew the places to look when doing some digging, there were always records of normal people, stretching back years.

Too many years, in the case of my aunts.

"What?" I muttered when I found myself faced with an

extraordinary timeline of bills paid and changes of addresses that made no sense at all. If I trusted these dates, Aunt Linda and Aunt Minerva were more like my great, great aunts. "They only look like they're in their late thirties or early forties," I muttered, wondering if there was something I was missing. Were there older generations who'd had the same names as them? In the end, I did the only sensible thing I could think of doing.

I asked them.

"How old are you both?" I asked, figuring that if they claimed to be the age they looked, I would then be able to broach the subject of what I'd found.

Ninety-eight? Give or take?" Linda said.

"One-hundred-and-ten," came Minerva's reply.

Then they both carried on sipping their tea, as though they hadn't just said something that had to be impossible.

"Plastic surgery?" I suggested, in a last ditch attempt to understand. I knew it wasn't, because their surgeon would have been world famous for solving all outward appearances of ageing, but I was out of logical explanations.

"Witches can have long and healthy lives when the proper preservation methods are practiced," Minerva explained, as though she were talking to a very dim three-year-old.

"Preservation methods?"

"She means we did a spell, so that we don't have to worry about wrinkles for a long time to come," Linda explained with a bright smile.

"It was all in the name of expanding our knowledge, so that we might have more time to spend on this earth to share it with those who need our help," Minerva informed me.

"It was for the wrinkles," Linda countered.

I sat down in a kitchen chair with a thump. Up until now, I'd been doing my best to look for logical alternatives to the strange things that kept happening to me. I'd believed that the chill of once having a curse aimed at me had merely been an overactive air-con unit. Hemlock talking to me was my imagination - and probably an undiagnosed disorder that I didn't want to investigate for fear of being called mad. Even the dog with the glowing eyes might have been caused by phosphorescent paint - like the Hound of the Baskervilles. But this little thing... this preposterous idea that my aunts were a good sixty years older than they looked... that was what was finally bringing the house of cards tumbling down.

"Can you prove it?" I asked, weakly. I was hoping that this was fake, or some kind of joke to fool me into believing something ridiculous.

"We have our birth certificates," Minerva began.

"We do?" Linda looked confused.

"Yes, we do. I confiscated yours fifty years ago, the last time you lost it."

"But I needed that!" Linda complained.

"Whatever for?"

Linda flicked her blonde hair away from an ear. "I wanted to collect my pension."

"Oh? And how were you going to do that?"

"Over the phone. They'd never have to know how well-preserved I am. I can do a great old person voice. Listen!" Linda pointed at her throat and made a few complicated motions with her fingers. "Pass the Wherther's Originals."

I nearly fell out of my chair in shock. It sounded so real.

Linda coughed and her voice returned to normal. "See? All of these years, I could have been getting free money!"

"Sure... until the day you turn one-hundred-and-twenty and the government realise you haven't died yet."

"I would fake my own death," Linda informed her older and wiser sibling.

"Do not listen to her, Hazel. That is not the witch way. We

do not take advantage of the extra years we have. We use them for the greater good."

"Right," I said, not really convinced by either argument that was being put before me. In fiction 'for the greater good' tended to mean that the person acting for the greater good was doing some really bad things that needed some kind of justification.

"Have they got any of that anti-aging potion lying around the place? Prevention is better than patching up the damage later," Hemlock said, slinking across the kitchen table.

"Have you been watching those adverts on TV again?" I called after him, but all I got back was a sulky 'No'. He was still a kitten, for crying out loud! Advertisers were abusing their position of power.

My aunts smiled at me, like I hadn't just imagined a conversation with my cat. It was a weird feeling. Finally, I couldn't take it any more.

"What is it you're waiting for me to do? I think I'm just normal, completely normal," I said, feeling incredibly disappointed for the first time. I didn't even know what I was missing, because I was missing it, but even though most of the self-professed magic users in town weren't my cup of tea, I hated not being in the smug magic club. I was missing out on something that everyone seemed to think was in my heritage.

"Give it time," Minerva assured me with an annoyingly calm smile.

"The longer it takes, the stronger the witch. I hit my powers when I was twenty-four. Minerva was twenty-five, the overachiever. Imagine what you'll be like when it happens! You'll be able to blink and turn that horrible high priestess into a snake," Linda assured me.

"But you won't do that, because all power comes with a responsibility… and a cost," Minerva warned.

"Phooey! What cost? All of that nonsense stopped when the Witch Council was turned into slime in that freak accident. No one stepped forward to take their place." Linda winked at me.

"And who turned them into slime?" Minerva folded her arms and glared at her sister.

"It was that or be prosecuted for misuse of magic!"

"And you thought the best solution was to misuse more magic?!"

"Yes. And it worked." Linda looked smug.

"Only because you hid the slime, so I couldn't turn them back."

"I didn't hide it. I sold it." Linda grinned at me. "Who do you think started that slime craze all the kids are so into?"

I discovered I was staring at the wood grain on the table without actually seeing it. "I think I should go and do some things around the shop," I muttered, my head filled with possibilities. Crazy possibilities.

Worst of all was the uncertainty. When you've believed something for your entire life, it is very hard to alter that belief - even when presented with strong evidence to the contrary. I was still looking for the cracks in the facade. This still felt like a twisted joke... and my life was the punchline.

"Yuck. Stop feeling so sorry for yourself. You're surrounded in a layer of doom," Hemlock remarked, slinking past to sit in his usual spot on the counter.

"Really? A real layer?" I asked, feeling my heart quicken for a beat.

"Nope. No magic here, Worst Witch. I'm still the laughing stock of the familiar community." Hemlock pressed his head down into his paw. "I had so much potential."

"That's it. Even writing this stupid article is better than thinking about all of this stuff," I said, pulling my phone out in a moment of decisiveness. I reached next to the till and found the card that Detective Admiral had left behind. *What can I tell him to get him to agree to talk to me?* I wondered, sifting through the evidence that Jesse and I had discussed.

In the end, I decided upon the blog and the business card. Hellion was no friend of mine, and even though Jesse seemed convinced he had nothing to do with the murder, setting the police on him sounded like payback - especially if he had been the one to vandalise the shop and post a curse through my letterbox. I may not be a part of their smug little witch club, but there was more than one way to boil a frog.

To my surprise, Detective Admiral sounded happy to hear from me. I definitely got the impression he was clutching at straws, and I'd just handed him a new one to hold. It must be tough going up against a man like Jesse Heathen - whose game I still hadn't figured out. The detective hadn't even minded when I'd asked if he could supply a quote for the article I was determined to finish writing. He'd even suggested we meet for tea... but not in Wormwood. It was one of Detective Admiral's brighter ideas.

Madame Rose's Tearooms in Hailfield was the kind of cafe you'd take your grandparents to for some good old-fashioned home-baking. When I entered the cafe I was immediately assailed by the delicious scent of baking wafting through from the back, and the remarkable display of cakes in the glass cabinet at the front.

"Good afternoon! How are you today?" a redhead with freckles greeted me. She had the sort of smile you couldn't help but answer with one of your own. Her name tag announced that she was Charlie Rose, which I deduced meant she owned the place.

"Let me take you through our specials. The cake today

was baked by our very own Lucy. It's a ginger and rum cake with lemon frosting. We also have a whole range of cakes from Black Cat Bakery, which is a fantastic place run by a waitress who used to work here, before she went on to greater things of her own," Charlie sparkled.

I found myself caught up in her enthusiasm. "A piece of that chocolate cake would be lovely," I said, pointing to a sticky looking cake that only had a couple of slices left.

"Excellent choice! It's made with the recipe that won the *Hobbling Cake Off* competition. You will not be disappointed." Whilst Charlie cut the cake, I found a table and waited for the detective to arrive.

I didn't have to wait for long. He walked in and greeted the owner of the cafe by name. She cut a second slice of the chocolate cake without even asking. I realised I'd discovered Detective Admiral's favourite haunt.

"Hazel, it's so good to see you," the detective began, smiling in a genuine manner.

"It's good to see you, too. Thank you for coming out when my shop was vandalised," I said, wanting to start the conversation on a good note.

"Don't mention it. It's my duty. I'm afraid we haven't made much progress towards finding the person responsible. Our time allowance for investigating things like that is constrained, due to budget shortages."

"I wouldn't expect it to be a priority, not when…" I trailed off, not wanting to rub the unsolved murder in his face.

He smiled, a little ruefully. "I'm going to be honest with you. The investigation isn't making much headway. I'm sure that's no great surprise to you, but I would appreciate it if you didn't share what I just said." He nodded to the notebook I was carrying.

"I'm not really a journalist, don't worry. It's just the local interest magazine. I'm not out to get a scoop," I assured him, pleased and surprised in equal parts that he seemed to be letting his guard down. Was there a chance he'd got over the frog incident?

"Glad to hear you're not one of those predatory journalists. I know we've all got to make a living somehow, but the morals of what they do…" He shook his head. "It has to be borderline illegal."

"Profiting from other people's misfortune? Unfortunately not," I replied, thinking about the way the world often seemed to spin on that very concept.

We both paused when our cakes arrived and took some time to enjoy those first few bites. And then a few more after that. It was an amazing chocolate cake.

"I brought the evidence I found with me. I was just doing some research when I happened upon it, and I wasn't sure if it might be helpful…" I said, taking out the print-out of the altar picture before the detective could ask me for it.

He reached out and touched my wrist with his hand. I looked up in surprise, straight into his serious grey eyes. "We have time enough for that later. I wanted to ask your opinion on something."

"Of course," I said, feeling hope flutter like a butterfly inside of my chest. I knew it was foolish to fall for a man who'd already tripped at the first froggy hurdle of my very strange life, but to say I was starved of options was an understatement.

I really needed to think of a better chat up line than that.

The detective reached into his bag and pulled out a folder. Then, without warning, he flipped it open. Brightly coloured pictures of the crime scene in all its gory detail spilled out across the table.

It was almost enough to put me off my cake.

13

CAKE AND CORPSES

"**T**hat's... that's a real dead body," I said, trying to get a grip on myself. I wasn't especially squeamish, but he had just sprung this on me without warning.

"Yes," the detective agreed, without apparently noticing my discomfort. "I was wondering if you might be able to take a look through and give me your opinion as a... er... as a local," he said, trying to avoid saying 'as someone who knows about weird stuff'. Because there was a lot of weird stuff in these photos.

I obligingly took the stack and attempted to focus on that, rather than the blood and the knife. *Gulp.*

As my eyes picked through the scene, I tried to view it all as facts, rather than feelings. My feelings had other ideas - but not in the way I was expecting. A sudden surge of strength rushed through me. I felt the hand of evil manipulating the scene I was being presented with. This was wrong... and someone needed to make it right. My eyes felt strange, and for one weird moment, I thought I saw an amber glow reflecting off the glossy surface of the photographs.

The next second, it was gone.

"See anything interesting?" the detective asked, focused on his cake.

He hadn't noticed anything happen, but that was probably for the best. A plague of frogs was one thing, glowing eyes were something else entirely. Anyway, I couldn't be sure of what I'd seen. The January sun was low in the sky, and there were lights on in the cafe. I angled the photograph this way and that, trying to replicate the glow I'd seen. It was while I was doing this that I noticed what was actually in the picture… what hadn't been publicised by the police.

On and around the body were spell bags, some spilling open to show herbs falling out of them. There were also tarot cards, tea leaves, silver coins, poppets, voodoo dolls, tiny bones, and grey dust - that I knew was graveyard dirt.

There really was something for everyone. If you believed in the power of all of this hoodoo and magic, the dead man should have been dead ten times over. But I didn't think the killer had wanted to curse this man to death. They'd taken a far more direct and pointy route by using a knife - a knife that I recognised as being the same type Hellion sold. For once, I wasn't keen to point the finger his way - mostly because I knew I wasn't above suspicion myself.

"That bag… the one with the herbs. It's from my shop. It's a hex bag," I said, pointing to the little black sack, which had spilled everywhere.

"Do you remember who you sold it to?" the detective asked. I got the impression it was a question he'd repeated many times and had yet to receive a satisfactory answer.

I shook my head. "I didn't sell it. My mother must have done… but it would have been a very long time ago. I don't sell hexes anymore." Even though I had never believed in them, the idea of selling nasty spells had always seemed twisted to me. You were essentially profiting from one person's anger, and - potentially - another's misfortune. I knew that I sold herbs that could be used to make the spells from scratch, but I'd conveniently decided that part was out of my hands.

I looked at the picture again. "These are all things from different traders in Wormwood. It's almost as if the killer wanted to point the finger at everyone." I raised my gaze and discovered the detective had lifted an eyebrow.

"You're sure you didn't all go out into the forest together to kill a stranger? It would make a change from the usual village picnic."

I wasn't sure if he was being serious or not. "I think someone is out to get the town... or rather, the part of the town who believe in the supernatural."

He nodded. "That is the conclusion I have been leaning towards. However, it hasn't made the investigation any simpler, especially when it may be that this murder had no personal motives whatsoever. The victim might have been primarily selected in order to confuse us, whilst damaging the community."

"That's a good theory." I was impressed by the detective's astuteness. I had been concerned that he would be blinded by Wormwood's weirdness and would take this murder at face value. Even I'd been guilty of focusing on the worst people our small society had to offer.

"I'm glad to know ten years of training and experience weren't for nothing," the detective said, deadpan, but I thought I saw a glimmer of amusement in his grey eyes. He was a hard man to read. "Although, lately, I feel like my competence is being questioned."

I winced, knowing he was talking about the mayor's unusual appointment of Jesse Heathen. "I'm sure Mayor Starbright was just trying to help," I said, for want of some-thing useful to add. The truth was, I had no idea why the mayor had decided to get involved at all. Gareth Starbright was an accountant. They weren't exactly famed for making exciting and surprising decisions. "Maybe he knows you're stretched pretty thinly because of your budget constraints?" I tacked on, thinking that it had to be the most likely cause of this otherwise out of character action.

"Perhaps. But it's not helpful at all. It's just added new levels of confusion, and the ridiculous idea that we are in competition." The detective balled his fist up and gently brought it down on the table in a controlled expression of frustration. "I just want to catch the person, or persons, responsible, and bring them to justice. That's the whole reason why I joined the police - not for fortune, fame, and a theatrical stage show," he said, practically spitting the last words.

Someone had certainly ruffled his feathers.

He raised his eyes to mine again. "That's why I wanted to meet with you today... to ask you a question I think you can answer for me."

I ignored the sinking feeling inside and put on my most helpful smile. "I'd be happy to help."

The detective nodded. "Has anyone new come to town recently? Either before or soon after the murder?"

I opened my mouth to say no, of course not, but the words stuck in my throat. I knew of two new people in town who had turned up one day after the murder.

My aunts.

I bit my lip and then realised I had to tell the truth. It would be worse if I didn't. Anyway, I didn't truly believe they'd had anything to do with this murder, did I? A small voice in my head whispered that I didn't know much about them, and the little I had found out seemed nonsensical and impossible. Others in town seemed to recognise them, but years had passed since they were last in Wormwood. Did I really know who they were? I reassured myself that, if they were innocent, nothing bad would happen to them. They could certainly handle themselves when it came to the police, and honesty was the least suspicious policy in this situation. I told the detective the truth and he made a note of it.

"They believe they're witches, don't they?" he asked.

The frog incident had definitely not been forgotten.

I nodded, wondering if I was really doing the right thing. It certainly didn't feel that way. Nothing about this case felt right.

"Thank you. And thank you for this." The detective lifted the printout I'd given him. He hadn't seemed all that interested in the revelation that Hellion Grey had lied about not knowing the victim, but after our conversation, that did make sense. The detective believed it was just another false lead that the real killer had known we would find and follow. That much was something I was starting to see myself, but the rest of it didn't feel right. I may not have known my aunts for long, but I liked to think I was able to judge the characters of those who were actually living with me. For all their weirdness and their strange tales about the past, I did not believe they were killers.

Apart from maybe Linda, but in a non-malicious sort of way.

I couldn't believe I was even considering the slime story as possibly being true.

When I shook myself free from my thoughts, the detective had paid his half of the bill and was standing up to leave.

"Good luck in your investigation. What can I use for the magazine?" I asked, remembering that had been the deal.

He reached into the folder and pulled out a closeup of the scene - one that showed all of the little items, but none of the blood. "You can print this. Use it on the front cover, if you like. We've got all we need from it."

"Thanks," I said, not entirely sure I meant it. Whilst I appreciated the detective taking the time to come and meet me, I strangely felt a little bit used… and misled. Couldn't he have just met me at the police station, or anywhere less date-ey than this cute little tearooms?

"No problem. I'm sure you can come up with a decent quote. Something like 'the investigation is ongoing, but progress is being made.'" He nodded, apparently happy with his composition.

I tried to look pleased by this piece of nothing. "I hope you catch the culprit soon," I said, before watching the detective walk out of the cafe after waving goodbye to the owner and not bothering to even say farewell to me. I'd definitely struck out with the detective. Even the redheaded tearooms owner was shooting sympathetic looks my way.

I sighed and tried to decide whether or not to just have done and order another piece of cake. Heaven knows I needed something to soothe the burn of rejection. Whilst I was considering whether to opt for the special, or a brownie, a woman walked in carrying a stack of cake boxes. She placed them on the counter and called the owner over. I was admiring her white-blonde hair, when she turned and looked at me with her pale blue eyes. Something inside me seemed to lurch forwards, like it was being tugged towards this mystery woman. I stayed in my seat, startled by the feeling. For a moment, the box deliverer frowned in my direction, but then she gave her head a little shake and left the shop.

I walked up to the counter to pay and get a second slice of something to takeaway. I'd decided I wasn't going to hang around here moping. I had an article to write, and a life of solitude to be getting on with.

"That was January, the one who baked the cake you were eating. She's like a superstar around here! Everyone loves her cakes. She has a loyal following like you wouldn't believe."

Charlie rested her head on her hand for a moment and looked a tiny bit perplexed. "They do say that the student often outdoes the master, eh? But some days I wish I had even half a slice of that success!" She grinned at me. "What am I like? Spouting rubbish as usual! Thanks," she said when I tipped her and received my slice of the special. "You have a good day!"

"You too," I said, feeling slightly cheered by Charlie Rose's words. I knew the feeling only too well. You tried as hard as you could to make a business successful, but someone else was always doing better than you were. It was easy to get jealous when, in truth, we all needed to keep our eyes down on our own paper. Success was about us, not someone else.

But I was definitely not successful. Not by anyone's standards.

I walked out into the cold January evening. Snow had yet to grace us with its presence this year, but the winter's bite was as harsh as ever. I wrapped my coat tightly around myself and walked back across the recreation ground to where I'd left the car. I was passing by the play area when I heard someone talking.

I stopped walking. I recognised that voice.

With a strange sense of fate tugging at my strings, I crouched down and crept through the bushes surrounding the edge of the play area. *If the police could see me now,* I thought sarcastically. Jesse Heathen was sitting on a bench a little way from the bushes. I could see the smug smile on his face from my hiding place.

"Yeah, I've been watching him. He doesn't have a clue. He's eating up my leftovers."

Jesse did not sound like the smooth charmer I'd spoken to the other day. Worse than that... I thought I knew exactly who he was talking about.

Jesse Heathen can take a running jump! I thought, pretty

peeved that I'd been used, and was apparently still being moved around like a pawn.

"You keep doing your job. This will be wrapped up in no time at all. Remember who got you where you are today," Jesse carried on, and then let out a sharp laugh. "That's right. This is the favour, and it's over when I say it's over. I don't expect to be contacted again."

I watched as he pressed a button to end the call. Then, for one terrifying moment, he seemed to pause, as if in thought. His head turned towards the bushes. I held my breath, hoping that the approaching darkness meant I was more concealed than the man standing out in the open. After a tense moment passed, where I was strangely tempted to throw myself out into the open and confess everything I'd heard, Jesse got up from the bench and walked away into the night.

I waited until I couldn't hear his footsteps anymore and then I emerged from my hiding place.

Jesse Heathen wasn't the man he was pretending to be.

"Shocking," I muttered, sarcasm so strong I could have won the sarcasm Olympics. I'd known there was something too good to be true about all of that charm and charisma. Now I saw it for what it was - an act.

I considered everything I'd heard in that conversation and wondered how I could play it to my advantage. Jesse was watching Detective Admiral in order to find out how well he was doing in the case. For some reason, he wanted to be the first to solve the murder. I had no idea why it mattered so much. But I'd learned something far more interesting than that from the conversation I'd overheard. It was pretty clear that Gareth Starbright hadn't asked him to come to town to solve the case.

Jesse Heathen had the mayor on a leash, and he was tightening the collar.

14

THE SEE-THROUGH SPELL

I found myself in the back garden the next morning. It was Sunday, and somehow, I'd managed to wake up, shower, get dressed, and get a cup of coffee down me before realising I was conscious. Now I was standing out on the frosty lawn looking at the sparkling grass.

Why had I come out here?

Oh, right. To look for footprints.

In a world that felt like it was in the process of being tipped on its head, looking for footprints seemed like the logical thing to do. I walked to the edge where the flowerbeds started and tried to remember exactly where I'd seen Hedge and the dog disappear. I could see cat paw prints in the soil. Next to them, were a larger set.

There really was a dog, I thought. I wasn't sure if that was better or worse than finding out it had all been in my head.

"Was it *just* a dog?" I mused aloud.

"Not unless they're selling glowing red contact lenses for dogs. I'd say it's unlikely, but you'd be amazed what you can find on the internet these days…" Hemlock popped out from under a nearby bush.

"If I find out you've been using my PayPal account again, I'll ground you for a week!"

"Try it and I'll leave something dead in one of your drawers... and I won't tell you which one," Hemlock retaliated.

Was it just me, or was having a talking cat way worse than having a teenager?

"Anyway, it's not my fault you use the same password for everything." He casually licked a paw as he said it.

I made a mental note to check my account and cancel everything. And also learn some new passwords. I was a grownup. I could definitely remember more than one... right?

"Why was Hedge talking to a glowing dog?" I mused, just as the big kitten himself slid out from beneath another bush. I looked across at him, wishing there was a way I could understand. "Have you tried asking?" I said to Hemlock.

"He's a private cat. You can't just ask these things..."

I rolled my eyes. That was Hemlock's way of saying he didn't have a clue. Still... if there really had been a dog, then Hedge was clearly able to communicate with something. All things considered, I could understand why he didn't talk to Hemlock. If only I'd been smart enough to not answer back the first time he'd spoken to me...

"Another mystery that's going to have to stay unsolved," I observed.

"I have some ideas! I think it was a hellhound, and Hedge is selling us all in exchange for riches and power." Hemlock's tail waved around in the air, showing he was pleased with himself for coming up with this idea.

"Let me guess... it's what you'd have done if you were him?"

"I'm just furious that he got there first," Hemlock agreed.

In the end, I abandoned both Hemlock and the garden investigation as another lost cause. On the plus side, it made the prospect of trying to finish the article on the murder practically an enjoyable one.

Once I forgot all about the characters in the story I was writing, and just wrote it, the words came out just fine. I used facts, not feelings, and I presented the case as it was. There were no hidden agendas and no undercurrents - even though I had good reason to be angry at more than one of the players. This article wasn't about me. It wasn't for me. It was for Wormwood, and I was not going to use my magazine for propaganda.

I finished the first draft of the article and then flicked over to the image I'd scanned in, courtesy of Detective Admiral. I was going to stick with the photo I'd snapped in the woods as the image on the front cover, but this would be good within the article. I thought that the detective had known he was giving me a dud - a collection of items that had the potential to offend, rather than intrigue, if placed on the cover. The old Hazel might have said that was paranoia talking, but after everything I'd been through these past few days, I wasn't discounting anything, or anyone. Everyone seemed to have an agenda when it came to the murder of Zack Baden.

I enlarged the picture, so it was way bigger than it would be printed, just to check that the quality was okay. Everything looked crisp. I'd done a good job of scanning it.

I was about to zoom out when I realised I was looking at the contents of one of the collection of spell bags, which had spilled out over the forest floor. What I'd initially dismissed as powders and herbs were in fact…

"Rose petals and hibiscus," I muttered. I had both in stock and had no doubt that, much like everything else that had been tossed into this image, they had likely originated from Wormwood. I regularly sold those two ingredients and knew they were popular with the local witches... after Jesse Heathen had come to town, I'd even sold out.

I sat back in my chair.

It didn't make any sense.

In a collection of curses, hexes, voodoo, and horror, why had someone tossed in a spell bag full of love spell? Especially a love spell that had been ripped apart. If it weren't for that detail, I might have been able to put the bag's presence down as a mistake - much like the horror-film ad-libbing. But this... this was deliberate. It was probably the only deliberate thing in the whole collection of magical paraphernalia.

As I looked at the broken love spell, one word came into my head: revenge.

It had been playing on my mind ever since I'd gone to the coven meeting with Jesse, and he'd laughed at the idea of this having anything to do with Hellion and Natalia.

I'd wondered about this possibility from the start, but that had been when I'd thought the other visitors were dead. Now I knew they wanted to stay missing.

It was the strangers. The man and the woman who had come to town with Zack Baden. The man and the woman no one could quite remember. It made sense if they were the killers, and now I thought I might have found the motive.

Zack Baden had worked with both Hellion and Natalia. I had definitely sold Natalia those very ingredients several times over, prior to the murder. If I were going to guess what kind of spell work she sold - especially spell work with the added extras that Jesse Heathen had implied - I would have guessed love spells. That was just like Natalia, helping people to mess with other people's lives when it definitely wasn't the right thing to do.

I had no idea if Hellion's work had been included

amongst all of the dark magic stuff, but a blade from his shop had done the deed. At first, I'd considered their guilt, and next, I'd been thinking they were being framed - like everyone else in town - but in truth, I thought they were the reason this murder had taken place in Wormwood. Whoever Zack Baden had targeted with the spells he'd bought, I thought they'd found out about it... and they hadn't been happy.

But why kill him in such an elaborate manner and try to point the finger at an entire town? I wondered. All I could think was that the couple I now believed were the killers had hated the place that had aided their enemy. It was a little weak and wobbly when it came to the motivation for leaving false leads, but it was all I had. If I could locate the missing couple, then I'd be able to ask them about it. *Or rather, the police will be able to ask,* I thought. I was just a humble magazine writer getting some fresh research for an article. If I found anything concrete, I would be telling the police, but I knew they needed evidence... and someone had to gather that for them, right?

"Where are you?" I muttered, still mystified about the couple no one could seem to remember, and no one had been able to find.

I found myself back on the internet, trawling through social media sites. I wasn't certain that Zack would be connected to them. After all - that was a sure way to tie yourself to murder. But I had to look. There had to be something I'd missed.

I flicked through all of the old photos where Zack was with a group of people. I made certain to look at every single person's face and note every name - although few were tagged. I wasn't sure what I was waiting for, but something inside me whispered that I would know it when I saw it. The little voice said to look harder.

So I did. I zoomed in on every image until the pixels nearly blurred. I studied them, wondering what I was missing. Just when I was about to give up, something caught my eye. It was a blur. At first, I thought it was just a blur of light, some kind of trick made by a reflection, but then I tried to focus harder on the blurry spot... and I couldn't. It was like looking into a dense mist. I got the strong sense that I wasn't supposed to be looking here, I shouldn't look at this blur. I blinked and tried again. This time, I realised they were faces... filmy, and hard to focus on, but I thought I'd seen enough to be able to recognise them. That was more than anyone else in town could claim.

I sat back in my chair and let out the breath I didn't realise I'd been holding. I had found them. They had been hiding in plain sight all along.

It didn't take long to search the friend lists of the other people tagged in the photo and find the identity of the blurred couple. They might have unfriended Zack, but they were hardly hiding their identities. The pictures on their profiles were normal. They hadn't expected anyone to recognise or remember them. Daniel Peates and Jasmine Everett - those were the names of the couple I believed had killed Zack Baden.

"Ouch," I said, feeling a sudden headache hit me. It felt like there were needles behind my eyes, trying to poke their way out the front.

"Hazel, do you know where the vacuum cleaner is? Your Aunt Minerva has stolen my stash of romance novels and won't tell me where they are until I vacuum up the summoning circle I was working on last..." Linda gasped and dropped the cup of tea mid-sentence when she saw me sitting there clutching my head. "Your eyes..." she said, before rushing over and hugging me.

"I think I'm dying," I told her, still holding my head and adding suffocation by hug to my current list of troubles.

"You just used magic, didn't you?" Linda looked delighted. "Drat. That means I have to pay Minerva."

I managed to peer out from behind my hands. "You betted against me being a witch?"

"Of course I did! You just seemed so nice and normal. Take it as a compliment."

All things considered, I decided that I would. I hadn't exactly been overwhelmed by the general niceness of the magical community. "I don't think I used magic," I muttered, but I wasn't entirely sure that was true. I'd made blurs turn into people, and I couldn't shake the feeling that I'd somehow seen through a spell that had been keeping their identities secret all along. *Who put the spell on them?* I wondered, but was attacked by fresh headache pains.

"Look at your eyes," Linda whispered, pulling me to my feet so I could look in the ornate mirror that hung on the opposite side of the shop.

They were glowing bright amber.

"That's impossible," I muttered, but I knew the time had finally come for me to accept it. This was undeniable proof of everything I'd been ignoring for so long.

Magic was real.

And I was a witch.

"Things are going to start happening now. You'll see," Linda said, standing next to me and looking as proud as a mother hen.

That doesn't sound ominous at all, I silently thought.

A ROCK AND A HARD PLACE

After Linda had told Minerva the happy news and both of them had praised my (as yet) still non-existent abilities, I asked their opinion on the spell that had triggered my headache, and they obligingly took a look.

"I can't do it. It will give me wrinkles if I squint that hard," Linda announced after two seconds of trying. Even Minerva seemed unable to focus.

"This is strong magic. We all have our different abilities. Neither of us are good at unravelling spell work. We're spell weavers," she told me. "You must be different."

"That's her way of saying she can't do it either," Linda smugly filled in.

I flipped back to the profiles where the couple were fully visible. I was going to click off again, and see if I could find any record of an address, when Minerva reached out a hand and stopped me from clicking.

"Wait. There's something wrong with that man."

"Oh, oh no," Linda said, looking over my shoulder.

"What?" I asked, looking back and forth between them.

"He's been cursed," Linda said.

"At least, he had been in this photo. It is just a snapshot in time. There are traces of it all around. A nasty curse, too," Minerva agreed.

"What about the woman? Can you tell if she's under a spell?" I asked.

Minerva shook her head. "No, but it doesn't mean that she isn't. Curses - the really bad ones - are fairly easy to spot, if you know what you're looking for."

"That makes sense," I said, swiftly joining up the dots. "The curse must have been from Hellion for this man, Daniel... and the love spell..."

"...for his fiancée," Minerva finished, pointing to the relationship status on Facebook. People really did share everything online these days.

"That's terrible," I said, before remembering that this couple had paid Zack back for his attempted breakup in an even more terrible way. Two wrongs did not make a right. "I think they found out what he'd done. That's why they killed him."

It was too bad I had zero proof.

"Good luck," Linda said, smiling and slowly backing away.

I frowned at my aunts. "What's the matter?"

"We can't interfere with this. By witch law, what they have done is fair play - if the victim really did try to curse and bewitch that couple," Minerva explained.

"But what about..." I'd been about to say 'misuse of magic', but Zack had been the one to misuse it.

"Our laws..."

"Guidelines," Linda interrupted.

"Laws," Minerva corrected, "are quite severe. And for good reason!" She glared at her sister. "We should not interfere."

"But this is more than just a murder," I argued. "This move was against the whole town. I understand why this couple was angry, but they've deliberately tried to make this about everyone in Wormwood - everyone who practices some kind of magic."

"There is nothing we can do. It would just be further misuse of magic," my aunt informed me, before shooting a warning look at her wayward sister. "But that doesn't mean you can't do something. Just not anything magical."

"No chance of that happening," I muttered. So far, my only powers were glowing eyes and splitting headaches.

"Don't speak too soon. You're at a pivotal time in your life as a witch. You need to be careful," Minerva warned.

"This is so exciting. I'm going to pick a good hex you can try out on that enemy of yours... Natalia, wasn't it? She will never try to curse you again," Linda announced, before running off towards the kitchen.

"Linda!" Minerva called after her, before following with swift strides.

I smiled and looked back at the screen.

"Well, if it isn't Sabrina the Middle-age Witch." Hemlock jumped down onto the desk where I was working.

"Middle-age?! I'm in my twenties!"

"Late twenties."

"Mid-twenties," I countered.

Hemlock swished his tail. "So... it finally happened. My talents aren't going to waste after all. I'm so proud. I think I'm actually choking up a bit." He made a strange coughing sound. "My mistake. It's a hairball."

"Out!" I said, shooing the hacking feline through the shop door and out onto the street. It wasn't that I didn't mind cleaning up after my pet cat, but he liked to aim for things that he knew were hard to clean - like all of the stock for the shop. With a normal cat, you could pretend that they didn't know what they were doing. But Hemlock liked to boast.

With the cat out of the way and my aunts doing... something… I got back to my internet search. It turned out to be a piece of cake to find an address for my suspected murderers. Jasmine had an at-home pottery painting business, which conveniently told me the exact address I needed to go to. With the thrill of the breakthrough running through my veins and the headache fading away, I left the house, jumped in my little VW Up!, and started driving towards the village of Hobbling.

It was time that someone got justice for the town of Wormwood.

It was only when I pulled up by the kerb a little way from the house that I realised I didn't have a plan. With the spell making this couple's connection to the victim invisible, and their faces scraped from the memories of all who had seen them with Zack, I knew it was going to be an up hill battle to prove them guilty of anything.

I wasn't even sure that I was right about all of this - about any of this.

That was the first thing I needed to fix.

With the barest of plans forming in my mind, I walked up to the house and rang the bell.

A woman I recognised as Jasmine Everett opened the door dressed in a paint-stained apron. She looked like someone's cheery mum and not a stone-cold killer.

"Can I help you?" she asked with a smile on her face.

"This is a little strange," I began, hesitantly, "but I was driving past and sensed a concentration of negative energy around this house. Do you know if you, or a partner, might have been cursed, or placed under a forced love spell?" I kept my smile light and breezy.

Jasmine turned white.

"What is it, honey?" Daniel called, coming into view. I squinted at him and thought I could see... something. Perhaps he was under a curse after all.

I tried not to freak out about just how nuts that was.

"It's nothing," Jasmine said and slammed the door in my face.

I stood on the step for a moment longer, before turning and walking back down the path. *Was that it? Is that all you can do?* my brain mocked me. I had come here and found out that all of my theories about the case were probably correct, but I didn't have anything even resembling proof. No one would remember this couple. No one would be able to tie them to Zack Baden. *No one normal,* I mentally amended, thinking for a moment of Jesse Heathen. But there was no way I was going to involve him - not when it was clear he had an agenda of his own.

Instead, I did what any sensible and rational person would do in my situation. I sat and moped in my car.

I was just beginning to wallow in self pity when I saw the front door of the house open. In a blind panic, I pressed myself down as low as I could in the car. In a car the size of the one I owned, it meant I was giving a contortionist a run for their money and might need the fire brigade to get me out again. With just my eyes poking up over the window sill, I checked to see what they were doing.

The couple looked pretty agitated. I could see the man, Daniel, arguing with his fiancée. She shouted something back at him, but I wasn't able to catch it. She threw her hands up in the air and they got into the car, looking every bit as shady as I now knew they were.

I couldn't believe my luck when they drove away from the house. This was my chance to find evidence - irrefutable evidence that they were guilty.

I got out of the car and hesitated. Was I really going to

break-in to a house in order to find something worth finding? If I was caught, I could go to prison. Or worse - be fined lots of money I definitely didn't have! "It might help your reputation," I muttered, thinking that being known as a little bit crazy was no bad thing in Wormwood. That was - if Wormwood survived its current PR nightmare.

"Let's warmup with trespassing," I said, deciding that the carport was the best place to look first. I honestly had no idea what 'evidence' would even look like, which made it that much more surprising when I found it almost immediately.

"No way..." There was a can of grey paint - custom mixed, according to the label - just behind some cardboard boxes. The liquid had leaked down the sides of the can after being used, and as if that hadn't been enough, there were a couple of dowel rods lying next to it coated with dried paint.

The paint had bothered me ever since I'd seen it slapped all over the trees in the woods. The red spray paint made sense - red was the colour of warnings and evil things. All of the horror films used red. But the grey had been soft - stylish, even. And now I knew why. This paint had probably been left over from an interior decorating spree at one time or another, and this pair had been too dimwitted to realise it could be traced back to them. It was a unique shade. All the police needed to do was seize the can of paint, analyse it to get a match, lift some fingerprints, and they would have enough evidence to start applying some real pressure on Jasmine Everett and Daniel Peates.

I pulled out my mobile phone and called Detective Admiral. Even as I was telling him about what I'd found, I discovered I couldn't take my eyes off the dowel rods. I reached over and picked one up, inspecting it more closely.

"I've got to go. I hope you can bring them in and get them to confess," I said, hanging up before the detective could tell me to wait where I was.

There was something that I needed to check.

After my spot of trespassing had been successful, I hadn't expected to be graduating to full-on breaking and entering… and at a completely different location.

I waited in the silence that seemed to hang in the wake of the click of the lock and the creak of the door when I let myself in to the house. As breaking-in went, it had been a piece of cake. It was amazing how many people thought that hiding a key under a rock - when it was the only rock in the vicinity - was a good idea. It had taken me two seconds to find it.

Nothing made a sound. The house was dark and apparently empty.

I made my way along the corridors, trying to remember the layout of the property. Where had I been? I turned left and discovered the room I was searching for.

The night had drawn in and moonlight filtered through the large bay window. I was only too conscious that I was probably very visible from the road. The only thing in my favour was that it was a private road that didn't lead anywhere in particular.

I lifted the dowel rod with the paint on it and placed it against the wall. Then, I turned on the torch on my mobile phone, squinting through the bright light.

It was a perfect match. I had found the real mastermind behind the murder.

The light snapped on in the room.

I spun round and discovered there was a man standing in the doorway.

"What are you doing here?" Grant Kingsley asked me.

16

SAVED BY THE BELL

"I ... I remembered how much I loved the colour you painted this room. Monochrome looks amazing in a house like this. I was thinking of redecorating but just couldn't wait? I didn't think it would be hurting anyone if I just popped in for a second?" I tried a nervous smile.

Grant looked about as impressed as my terrible story warranted. Which wasn't very. "You know... don't you?"

"Know what?" I wasn't quite finished with the amateur dramatics. If there was anything I could say to convince him that I really didn't know what he was talking about, I was going to say it.

"You know about the paint. I suppose it was sloppy, but then... I never expected those two to be found by anyone. How did you trace them, by the way? I used a very strong spell..."

"You used a spell?" I said, stunned by this revelation. "I thought you hated the weird side of Wormwood!" We'd had a whole conversation about it when I'd come to look for places for my aunts to stay.

"Oh, I do," he said, considering the dowel rod I was holding.

I tightened my grip. It was the only weapon I had. "I should have known it wasn't those two who were responsible for everything. This wasn't just about personal vengeance. It was about making Wormwood look bad. Why?" I frowned. I hadn't yet figured out that last part.

Grant smiled, his teeth looking sharp in the soft glow of the lightbulb. "That is my business. All I want to know is how did you trace my attack dogs?"

"And then what? You'll let me go?" I wasn't about to trust a single word this man said.

Grant Kingsley laughed. "Of course not. I'm going to kill you."

"The police know about Jasmine and Daniel. They're probably telling them all about you right now." He had to know this was over. It might be my only way out of here.

"Thank you kindly for the warning. I'll be sure to make preparations before they get here. From the look of that piece of wood in your hand, all you have on me is some sloppy paintwork. With hindsight, I should have bought them some new paint, but it was left over. And honestly, I thought it would add a touch of class to proceedings. Red is so garish and clichéd, don't you think?" He took a step towards me. I immediately moved the same distance backwards. I didn't know what Grant Kingsley had planned, but I already knew what he was capable of.

"You wanted everyone to look in the wrong direction and point fingers at one another. You wanted the town to tear itself apart and forget they ever saw the real killers," I said, trying to subtly circle around Grant whilst he inched closer still.

"Tell me something I don't know…"

"Were you the one who did those things to the pigeons

and rats... and my shop?" I added, wondering how much handiwork the landlord had put in.

That insane grin never shifted. "No one notices the familiar faces around town. I could have done it even without my little trick and got away with it."

"I still don't understand. If you have so much power... Wormwood should be your home, your community..." I thought about how Grant had always been up on his hill, looking down at the town. Even though everyone knew and respected him, he'd never been involved in Wormwood's affairs, and no one would ever have suspected him of having a secret of his own.

An image flashed through my mind. A memory from the day of our meeting swam to the surface. I'd seen something on Grant Kingsley's desk... pictures of properties he owned and some impressive modern-looking property developments. "You wanted to sell off Wormwood for a profit... but no one was buying," I finished, finally understanding everything that I had seen and learned.

Grant looked surprised for a second, but then he brought his hands together in a slow clap. "I don't know if you're one of the few genuine psychics this town has, or something else entirely, but I'm impressed. You'll understand. You've lived in this town for most of your life. Does anything ever change?"

I shook my head, as I was supposed to. We were still circling, and I knew things could escalate at any moment. I needed a better weapon than a thin piece of wood that would snap on the first impact.

"I've been renting out property for years. I've done well from it, I'm not denying that, but do you know what years of people complaining about rising rents and paying late does to you? Of course you don't. You probably think I'm complaining about nothing, and if I hate it so much, why not do something else? Here's the punchline - I can't. I am sitting on what would be a fortune's worth of real estate anywhere else in the South East of England, but in Wormwood, the prices are stuck forty years in the past! Nothing here ever changes. I've tried to counteract whatever hoodoo or spell it is that's keeping this place that way, but I can't touch it, or even find it! It was time to try something different."

"You wanted the town to destroy its magical community, so you could finally get your payout," I concluded.

"You're 100% correct. With the way things are going, half of the town is going to be locked up on suspicion of murder, and the rest are going out of business. You must have noticed people are struggling?"

I had. The influx of customers buying magical ingredients to bring prosperity and luck had been remarkable. With the exception of the bakery, I would have guessed that my business was currently experiencing record sales. But I knew it would end for me, too - if business in town really was dying.

"And you are going to help me to do it. Whilst we've been talking, I've been thinking. You've got me on the paint, but the police haven't visited this room. Even if one of them has dropped by to ask about property in the past, they're not going to remember the colour of the paint. Few people have your eye for detail. Sure, those fools might confess and might bring my name into it, but it's no big deal. Jasmine and Daniel have never been inside this house. They don't know where I got the paint from. The police will need a warrant before they search this place, which will give me more than enough time to put up a few rolls of wallpaper. I think cerise would look just as good in here, am I right?" He raised his dark eyebrows, as if we were having a normal conversation about interior design, and he wasn't planning to murder me.

"I think you just got greedy," I told him, before wondering what the heckity I thought I was doing. Was goading my would-be murderer really a good way to persuade him out of it? My peripheral vision had yet to find any suitable weapon upgrades for my deficient dowel rod. Curse these trendy people and their minimalist living spaces! If this encounter had taken place back home, I could have brained him with three pieces of semi-precious rock and an ugly plant pot by now.

"How did you even find two people who wanted to kill Zack Baden?" I blurted out when everything else seemed to be failing me.

"If you're here, then you've done your research. You should already know that Zack wasn't a nice guy." Grant sidestepped. I shrank back.

He seemed to relax for a moment, probably knowing that I was a rat caught in a trap. "I didn't pick Zack. His connection to Wormwood was actually just a happy coincidence. I had planned to fabricate all of that, but I didn't need to, did I? Daniel Peates rents a property in Wormwood that I own. Before you think that's an easy connection to me, I rent a lot of properties to a lot of people. And anyway, it's not him who lives there, it's his mother. Neither of them have paid rent for a few months. I was going to evict his mother - I'm not running a charity - when Daniel came in and said he would do anything, anything at all, if I just gave him some more time to get the rent together. That was when I finally saw the light at the end of the tunnel. I asked Daniel if there was anyone he wanted dead... and guess who's name he said?"

I shook my head. I wasn't going to play along.

Grant's smile faded for just a second. "Even people who don't live in Wormwood get done over by what happens in this town. He knew that Zack had done something, both to him and his girlfriend. Zack might have bought a couple of decent spells that actually worked, but he wasn't smart enough to hide them properly. Daniel and Jasmine found those little hex bags and they got scared." Grant laughed again. "It was too perfect, especially when I realised who they had come from." His eyes glinted. "Everyone in Wormwood is so desperate to show off their signature style. There are so many egos in play it was simple to point a few fingers and watch as the town did the rest. I couldn't believe it when I found out our dead man had been poisoned and seduced prior to his murder. Everything came up trumps... and things are only getting better."

I sensed that the little time I'd been gifted was up. Grant didn't want to chat any more.

"They will catch you," I told him.

"I doubt that very much. Just one last question... how did you see through that masking spell I used? It worked on everyone else in this hell hole of a town. I didn't think you were a witch."

"I'm not," I automatically replied, before biting my lip. "Or maybe I am." It really was now or never when it came to embracing what I was becoming - what I had always been.

Grant looked bemused. "Okay then. Still, I doubt you're witch enough to stand up to this." He pulled a small black bag from his pocket and shook it. I thought I heard bones clinking inside. Something about that little black bag made every hair on my body stand up on end. "This is like the nuclear bomb of magic. I'm sure you'll recognise Hellion's brand..." He pointed a long finger to the little quote that I knew would read 'A Nasty Piece of Work'. Grant did have a point when he said that the business people in town loved everyone to know their names... even when they were doing bad things.

"Curses don't always kill people instantly. They're supposed to make you suffer." Even I knew that much.

Grant looked from the bag to me and back again. "As I said, this curse is a nasty one, but you're absolutely right. Some things in magic take time to manifest. I'll be taking a quicker route." He pulled out a ceremonial knife - the same kind that had ended the life of Zack Baden.

"I'd say that Hellion is getting what's coming to him, if he sells his knives to anyone and everyone, but does he really not even ask what the things he sells are going to be used for?" I said, exasperated. I held the piece of dowel out in front of me, but I knew it was going to be about as useful as a chocolate teapot. It was just so typical that the day I'd discovered something about myself that might help me find my place in this world was also the day I was going to die.

"He does make it easy," Grant agreed. "I want you to know that you'll be helping the cause out a lot. One fewer business in town is going to be a big plus when it comes to letting the high street die. The second ritualistic killing of someone who's been resident in town since they were born is definitely going to tip the scales a lot more heavily in my favour. It's too bad you won't be around to see what Wormwood becomes when it joins the rest of South East England. I'll offer you a deal. If you make this easy and neat, I'll make this fast. I'd rather not have to clean up... not when the police are probably going to want to take a look around."

"No chance," I told him, tightening my grip on the piece of wood.

Grant shrugged... and then our deadly dance of death began.

"This is supposed to happen! It's meant to be," Grant hissed, ducking when I threw one of the small ornamental pots that decorated the sparse mantlepiece at him. It was too bad there were no pokers in sight. Then I might have stood a chance.

"If you believe that, then you really are crazy," I said, reaching for the second pot. Even the chromed stag's head was mounted too high to reach.

"You really don't see how this all fitted together? Everything has been perfect, even this. It's almost as if by magic." Grant Kingsley's eyes glinted for a moment.

I felt something rush past me. My eyes warmed and glowed in response. Grant had just tried to do something, but it didn't seem to have had any effect.

"I guess you really are a witch," he said, looking disconcerted for a second, before lunging at me with the knife. I grabbed his hand, trying to push the blade away. We went down together, landing heavily. Grant pushed himself to the top and tried to force down the blade. I could only watch as it inched closer and closer to my chest and the end became inevitable. *Magic... if you could save me now, I'll never ask for anything again!* I silently prayed, but I knew I didn't have the skills. I didn't have anything. I was going to die.

A sound like a gong being struck rung out.

I realised I'd shut my eyes when the blade had finally started to bite into my skin.

Was this death? Had I died? I'd been expecting it to hurt a lot more.

I opened my eyes. Grant Kingsley was on the floor, apparently out cold. The knife had fallen out of his hand and lay harmlessly on the rug, a small distance away. Standing behind him with a smile on his face was Jesse Heathen.

"Saved by the bell. Or in this case... the saucepan I grabbed on my way in." He pulled out a rather dented stainless steel pan from behind his back.

I'd never been so happy to see anyone, or a kitchen utensil, in my entire life.

17

THE SQUINT

"How did you know to come here?" I asked.

"A 'thank you' would be nice."

"Thank you. Why are you here?" I said, getting up and crossing my arms.

"I was in the neighbourhood and heard shouting." Jesse shrugged.

I shot him a disbelieving look, but he remained silent. Apparently that was all I'd be getting out of him. I decided it didn't matter. I knew Jesse was in town to pursue some secret agenda of his own, but right now, I didn't care what it was.

There was a sudden pounding on the door.

"Open up! It's the police!" came a shout.

Jesse and I looked at one another. We both knew that, if he hadn't been there, the police would have arrived just in time to find my body. Whilst that would certainly have been compelling evidence against Grant Kingsley, I was glad I wasn't currently a corpse.

I walked out into the corridor and opened the door to the police.

Sean Admiral frowned when he saw me. "What are you doing here? I'm looking for Grant Kingsley."

"He's in the front room. He just tried to kill me," I told the small force of police.

"Right," the detective said, nodding and trying to take that in. "You okay?"

I nodded.

"What is *he* doing here?" I heard one of the other officers mutter.

I looked round to discover that Jesse had followed me out of the room.

He smiled around at the unhappy police force. "You might want to get your criminal cuffed. He's starting to wake up. Or, I could hit him again, if that would be easier." He twiddled the saucepan handle in his hand.

"You hit him?" Detective Admiral looked like all of his Christmases had come at once, and not because he'd potentially solved a murder investigation.

"Nice try. It was purely heroic, as Ms Salem here can attest."

Detective Admiral looked at me hopefully, clearly wanting me to tell him that Jesse was nuts and definitely guilty of assault.

"He did save me," I grudgingly confessed.

"Such gratitude. I'm overwhelmed," Jesse commented, looking amused by the way everything was playing out.

"I've got him cuffed, Detective!" one of the officers called from the grey front room.

Detective Admiral looked from me to Jesse, and back again. "We caught Daniel Peates and Jasmine Everett when they came back home. It was only a few moments after we arrived and bagged the paint can you told me about. Once we had them in custody, they cracked pretty much immediately and started pointing fingers at Wormwood's biggest landlord. We thought it was probably nonsense, until the story about Daniel renting a property in town for his mother checked out. To be frank, we still thought they were a couple of cranks when they accused Grant Kingsley. Did he really try to kill you?"

"There's a dagger on the floor in the front room with my blood on it that says he did," I told him. I didn't think it had done much more than scratch me, but it had been a close call. "If you check the paint in the tin against the paint used on the walls in there, you'll find it's the same. I think Grant Kingsley is the one who had it made up." It had been some pretty posh-looking paint. That fact alone should have alerted me to the probability that Daniel and Jasmine had not been working on this alone. That and the way it had been clear as soon as I'd met them that they were hardly a couple of criminal masterminds with witch powers to boot. How had I been so naive?

"Did he, uh… mention why he wanted to kill you?" Detective Admiral asked, looking baffled by all of this.

"He wants to sell off the properties he owns in Wormwood to property developers, but no one wants to touch them. He thinks that the townspeople are putting investors off. His idea was to put everyone out of business and make the town's reputation even worse, so that it would essentially destroy itself and make it so new blood would come into the town."

"And a new, more expensive, Wormwood would rise from the ashes," Jesse finished with a dramatic flourish.

Detective Admiral looked singularly unimpressed. "What were you doing here tonight, *Detective?*" he sneered, before looking questioningly at me, too.

I glanced at Jesse. He shrugged at me.

"I wanted to check if I was right about the paint. I meant to knock and see if Grant was around, so I could sneak a look, but the spare key was left out in the open..." I confessed.

"It was under a rock," Grant said as he was led out of the front room in cuffs.

"Which was out in the open!" I protested.

"She was breaking and entering. I caught her and defended my property. I wasn't trying to kill her," the landlord said, trying to sound calm and collected.

I was glad that no one seemed to be listening.

"Are you both willing to testify that Grant Kingsley intended to end your life, Ms Salem?" Detective Admiral asked.

We both nodded.

The detective sighed. "Take him away and read him his rights," he instructed the police officers.

He waited until we were alone in the house.

I knew what was coming next.

"Taking the law into your hands is an incredibly irresponsible thing to do. The correct way to have handled this situation would have been to call the police, so we could search the premises and see if the facts checked out," the detective informed us.

"Grant Kingsley was going to cover up that paint as soon as his name was dragged into this business. He told me that himself. Anyway... I wasn't completely sure. I needed to check. I didn't know Grant wanted to take down the entire town!" I protested.

"Even more reason to not go charging in on your own. You didn't know what you were walking into, or who you were dealing with!"

"Hazel nearly getting killed means you now have enough evidence to put Grant Kingsley away - which you wouldn't have had if it were just a case of matching paint. I'm betting the two you have in custody have already confessed to their crimes?" Jesse pointed out. "This is win win, isn't it?"

The detective glared at him. "The police do not condone vigilante action. What were you doing here tonight, Mr Heathen? Hazel didn't mention that you were with her when she entered the property."

I noticed he'd used my first name. He was also drawing himself up taller to square off against Jesse Heathen. Any other time I might have been flattered by the idea that a couple of men might be trying to show off for me, but this was just annoying and unhelpful.

"I wasn't with her. I'd actually just figured out the case myself and came to call on your guilty man. I saw him through the window trying to stab Hazel, so I did what any person would do and tried to help her out." He gave a self-deprecating shrug.

Detective Admiral made no effort to hide his disdain. "You'd just 'figured it out'. How, exactly, did you do that?"

"The same as Hazel, probably. It was pretty obvious that the crime scene was a setup. I knew we were looking for someone with a hidden agenda against the town. If they were able to cover their tracks, they had to be pretty powerful... and have some kind of vested interest. There aren't many people in town who fit that description. Grant Kingsley is an outsider. He's never participated in any of Wormwood's affairs, and beyond renting out his properties to a lot of the residents, he doesn't have any stake in the town. It's obvious when you think about it." Jesse inspected his nails.

The detective glanced at me. Too late, I realised I was wearing my skepticism on my face. Not that it mattered. A toddler would have been able to see through Jesse's highly convenient story.

Detective Admiral turned to me. "I would have expected this kind of thing from him, but I thought you were more sensible. I know you care about your magazine, but getting carried away for a story has some serious consequences. Breaking and entering is illegal. Grant Kingsley could press charges."

"But he tried to kill me!"

The detective shook his head. "You haven't done yourself any favours. When you're asked to testify in court, this could go against you."

"Don't sweat it, Hazel. Everyone who's anyone has a criminal record." Jesse looked amused by this entire conversation.

"You could have assault charges brought against you!" The detective turned on him.

Jesse chuckled. "I doubt that will go down well with the public. Not after the mayor sings praises to my heroism, and the local press herald me as the man who stopped Grant Kingsley's coldblooded rampage."

"We'll see about that," the detective bit back, before looking at me seriously with his grey eyes. "I thought you were different."

I looked across at Jesse and then back at the detective. "I'm just the same as all of the other weirdos in Wormwood," I told him with a little smile that warmed me all the way through my body.

"Clearly," Detective Admiral said dismissively.

He turned to walk away, but Jesse stepped in front of him. "You're the one who's being shortsighted. You don't see what's in front of you. There's a whole world you're missing. Without Hazel, you wouldn't ever have found your killers or the puppet master behind everything. You should be thanking her."

"There is no excuse for breaking the law." Detective Admiral's face had taken on a reddish hue as he stared down his adversary. "You should both leave. Go back home, Hazel.

And Mr Heathen, I suggest you crawl back under whatever rock it is you slithered out from."

Jesse shrugged at me. "Don't take it too hard. I know that this whole thing has only been solved because of you. I can see that you're special, even if he can't."

For just a second, when the detective was looking away - probably contemplating some lawbreaking of his own, in the form of punching Jesse Heathen - Jesse's eyes glowed amber.

I focused and felt mine do the same in response.

A smile tugged up one side of Jesse's mouth. "Let's leave the detective to his investigation. I'll walk you home. Contact the mayor if you need me," he added in the direction of the detective. "He knows how to reach me."

Jesse turned and walked out of the front door, leaving Detective Admiral spitting feathers.

I gave the detective one last apologetic look, before I followed him. I wasn't impressed with either man, but even though he was obnoxious, Jesse had saved my life. And I wanted to know the truth about why he'd been 'in the neighbourhood'. No matter what Jesse may claim, I knew better than to trust him. He was up to something, and I wouldn't be much of a journalist if I didn't try to do some digging.

The walk home was pretty quiet. Jesse had asked me if I was okay, before batting away any and every question I tried to ask him with the promise that he would tell me everything, once we were safe and inside. When we were inside the shop, and I'd locked the door and discovered my aunts must have gone out, I waited for Jesse Heathen to tell me the truth.

And then when he didn't, I told him he'd better start talking, or I would set my aunts on him. He laughed at that.

"Aren't you able to do it yourself? I couldn't help but

notice things have started to happen for you. Congratulations. If tradition is to be believed, you're going to be quite a witch." He smirked, as if he knew something that I didn't.

"I have a lot of questions… and you are going to answer them," I told him. "Or maybe my first act of magic will be to do something horrible to you. Isn't it also true that new witches don't know how to control their powers?" Okay, so I had totally stolen that from every fictional magical universe ever, but it had to be true, right?

Jesse's continued smirk hinted otherwise. "Whilst I would love to see that, we do need to talk. I know you're wondering how I knew Grant Kingsley was the bad guy. I would have told the detective the truth… if I'd thought he would believe me." He raised his amber eyes to meet mine. "Some people are bad to the bone. They can hide it, both in normal and in magical ways, but if you know how to look, there comes a time when they can't hide it any more. Things go rotten all around them…" He pointed to a wilted Venus fly trap on the counter.

I folded my arms and looked unimpressed. I'd only forgotten to water it for two days! It wasn't rotten. "That's really the story you're going to go with? Bad vibes tipped you off?"

Jesse narrowed his eyes. After a moment's thought, he nodded.

"Oh, sure. That is *so* believable!" I muttered.

His mouth quirked up again. "You believe in magic, don't you? Why won't you believe what I'm telling you?"

"We both know you're lying. Let's be grownups and acknowledge that much. I don't know why you don't want to tell me the truth, but until you do, this conversation is over. I'm not talking to you."

Jesse looked even more amused. "I thought you had questions?"

"And I thought you had answers." I glared at him before trying something new… something unrelated to the murder I'd just solved. "Why do we have the same colour eyes? I've never seen anyone else's glow, either."

"I don't know the answer to that. I guess we must have a similar kind of magic."

"What kind of magic would that be, by the way?" I'd known Jesse was up to his neck in all of the weirdness in Wormwood.

"Baby steps. You can't even see magic yet, can you?"

"See magic?" I questioned.

Jesse grinned and sat down on the counter. "It's called witch sight. You remember when we were at that coven meeting talking to your two friends?"

"Not my friends," I immediately corrected.

"I knew they weren't any kind of big deal in the magical world because of what I saw with witch sight. It shows you magic, but if you know what you're doing, it can also give you an idea of how powerful a witch or a magician is."

"You're saying that they're not powerful?"

"Completely average. Below average, in Hellion's case. He trades off the dark arts because you can do a lot with crude spell work. Grant had one of Hellion's bags, didn't he?"

I nodded. I'd forgotten all about the curse. I wondered where it had gone.

"I could feel it. It was a nasty piece of work, as the label suggests, but Hellion's spells are nothing special. They're like using a hammer, when a sharp needle would do a much better job," he explained.

"I'll be sure to tell Hellion he's doing it all wrong next time he decides to curse me," I muttered. I knew he'd been the one to post the cursed envelope through my door.

Jesse considered me. "He'd be a fool to try it now."

"Are you at least going to tell me how witch sight works?" I was getting frustrated with the endless question dodging.

"It's pretty easy, once you get the hang of it. It's also called 'the squint', which probably gives you a clue. You're looking for something unseen. You know the way your eyes glow? It will be like that, only... mostly less spectacular. I think you'll be very surprised by who does, and who doesn't have magic in this town... and how much they really possess."

"If you and everyone else in town can see magic... how come no one knew Grant Kingsley could do all that spell stuff?"

Jesse shrugged. "We both heard him. He hates what this town is all about. I'm not surprised he used the gift he'd been given to conceal what he truly is. Concealment seems to be his forte, wouldn't you say."

I nodded, thinking about the blurred photographs and strange blank memories. "Hang on a minute... you just said 'we both heard him' talking about his plans for Wormwood. That was before he tried to stab me!"

"It was a second before I walked in!"

I folded my arms across my chest. "No it wasn't." I squinted hard at him, but couldn't see anything magical. Darn it. This was going to take some work, if Jesse Heathen could even be believed.

"Don't try to use the magic trick I just taught you on me. You think Grant Kingsley is the only one in town with something to hide?"

"So, you admit it! You are hiding something." I was thinking back to the phone call I'd overheard.

Jesse grinned. "It's smart. It means people underestimate you." He looked at something I couldn't see, just over the top of my head. "You should probably figure out how to do the same... and soon. But maybe not before you put the fear of the devil into all of your enemies in town. That coven will regret their choice to exclude you."

"How do you know they excluded me?"

"Aside from the way it's painfully obvious that Natalia Ghoul despises you? You're from a prestigious witch family, and yet, you're not in the coven. Simple."

I wasn't happy about it, but I could tell that I wasn't going to get anything else out of Jesse Heathen - if that was even his real name.

"Who are you?" I asked him.

He smiled, his white teeth looking bright in the dim light of the shop. "I am no one," he said and dissolved into shadows, leaving me alone and stunned.

18

THE COLOUR OF MAGIC

I stood in the empty shop for quite some time after Jesse had pulled his vanishing trick.

"Who tried to kill you?" Hemlock asked, striding past me with a sideways glance.

"Grant Kingsley. It's a long story," I told him, unwilling to recount the entire evening to a cat.

"Glad you don't want to tell it, because I don't want to hear it."

"Hemlock…" I said when he was about to slink away behind some cabinets.

"The ol' walkaway. Gets 'em every time."

I pursed my lips. "Do you know how it's possible for a person to disappear? I mean… in the magical sense. As in, here one moment and not the next."

"I'd say you need to learn to walk before you can run. Or in your case… crawl."

"Do you know anything?"

He inspected his claws. "Maybe. Let's just say I may have hypothetically been looking through some spell books belonging to your aunts to see if I could get anything to work for me… hypothetically."

I raised my eyebrows at him.

"Equally hypothetically, it didn't work. I'm a failure. A failure!" he said, sobbing into his paw.

There was a pop as something materialised from nothingness.

Hemlock looked at the item that had appeared next to him on the floor. "Your first act of magic, and this is what you do?"

I leaned over and looked down at what I'd apparently summoned into existence. "It's the world's smallest violin… and it's playing a song for you."

"Hilarious," Hemlock said, kicking the offending item away with his back foot. "You don't deserve an answer to your question."

"I'll give you ten cat treats." I knew that this was a negotiation.

"A whole bag… and some catnip," he countered.

"One bag, but no catnip. You can't be trusted with it," I said, knowing I was being played as a sucker.

"The joke is on you - I already have the catnip." Hemlock twitched his whiskers happily. "As I was saying, before you started with the magical jokes at my expense, it is possible. It's just very advanced magic that needs experience and planning, and is only used in extreme circumstances."

"Like making a dramatic exit?"

Hemlock blinked. "Really? Who did that? I might put in for a familiar transfer…"

"I'll confiscate your treats!"

"Noooo!" he said, running off to raid the cupboard.

"What's all the noise about?" Aunt Linda asked, walking in from the garden with Minerva hot on her heels. I could smell woodsmoke and wondered what they'd been doing.

"Just arguing with a cat," I muttered, still no less confused. I squinted in the direction of my aunts.

Nothing.

Wait.

The longer I focused, the more colours seemed to appear before my eyes. Aunt Linda was a dark swirling magenta, whilst Aunt Minerva was deep blue. I blinked and the vision was gone.

"You just used witch sight! Aren't you a quick study? Done anything else cool?" Linda said, walking over to my tea section and helping herself to a bag of 'Learn to Love Yourself' tea. She really didn't need it.

"I made a tiny violin appear," I said, struggling to keep up with all of this.

"Great! I'm sure there's a really good explanation for that," Linda said, waving the bag at me. "So exciting! Did you do anything else fun whilst we were out? There's blood on your shirt. Not judging! We've all done things we regret. Or don't regret." She winked at me.

I looked down at the mark. It looked like it had stopped bleeding. It really had only been a scratch. "I broke into Grant Kingsley's house, and he tried to kill me. He was the one who organised the murder and he was going to give me a similar end. He was trying to stop Wormwood from being so..." I shot an apologetic look at my aunts.

" ...weird?" Linda finished for me. "It's always been that way."

"That was his point. He said he was frustrated that the property he owns never goes up in value, in spite of the prices rising everywhere else."

"I think I can see his point of view," Minerva said, astounding me. "It must be frustrating to not see a return on your investment."

"Yikes. You're still sore about Black Monday, aren't you?" Linda said.

"Black Monday? Is that the name of a sale?" It did sound familiar.

"No. The 1929 stock market crash. Minerva lost a little bit of money…"

"Everything," Minerva corrected.

"Even though her stocks are now worth something kajillion, she still regrets not cashing in before the crash."

"Those stocks would be worth ten times more to me now, if I had sold them and just put the money in the bank!"

"As you can see, Minerva is actually a human with human flaws, like the rest of us. She just likes to pretend otherwise," Linda sniped.

"Just look at you, Hazel. Have you seen how your power is growing? I can't wait to see it when it's finished materialising!" Minerva said, ignoring her sister.

I turned to the mirror and squinted. After a while, a hazy colour started to appear around me - the way it had with my aunts. "It's gold," I said, looking at the swirls of sparkling light. It was incredible. Unbelievable.

I was a witch.

"Jesse said I should find a way to hide all of this."

"Oh, it's Jesse now, is it?" Linda raised her eyebrows at me.

I pulled a face. "It is definitely not like that. Can you believe he waited around whilst I was in trouble just so he could rush in and 'save me' at the most heroic moment?"

"Urgh, typical man. The next time you see him, you should get your own back. I know a really good recipe for turning people into slime…"

"I doubt it would be that easy. I think Jesse might be a magician of some sort."

"I knew there was a reason I liked him so much! He must

have been using some kind of charisma spell. What a sleaze!" Linda complained. "I should have been suspicious when Minerva got puppy dog eyes, too."

"So… he's been hiding his magic. That's hardly the mark of a trustworthy person," Minerva said, looking thoughtfully at me.

"I don't trust him. Back at that town meeting, he claimed he was here to solve the murder case because the mayor had asked him to come, but I think he was lying about that. I don't even know if he came to town because of the murder," I said. "I asked him questions about the case and about magic, but he won't give me any straight answers. When I thought I might be getting somewhere with him, he disappeared."

Linda's eyebrows shot up even higher. "Disappeared?"

"Vanished - minus the puff of smoke. But there were some shadows."

The witches exchanged a look.

"Ooh, he's powerful," Linda said with an excited smile.

Minerva shot her a warning look. "This man sounds like someone you need to be very careful around. He might want to lead you astray."

"Towards the dark arts?" I said, feeling a thrill of excitement that I might have to choose between the dark and light.

Minerva frowned. "That is not the way magic works. Have you not read any of the family spell books?"

"I've skimmed a few," I said, defensively. It had been on my 'to do' list for, you know, sometime next year…

"Look at you! A chip off the old block," Linda said proudly.

Minerva ignored her. "I'm sure everything will be straightened out in no time. You said the people responsible for the murders were caught, so I'm sure things will be a lot quieter around here. We can work on exploring your magic together. That kind of thing has always been a family matter.

No one from outside needs to interfere." She looked over the top of her glasses at me.

"That's fine. I don't care if I never see Jesse Heathen again," I said, feeling like a teenager who'd been caught sneaking home at the dead of night. Not that I had ever done that as a teenager. I'd been as strait-laced as they came. My mother had been so disappointed…

"Did nothing happen when the man was trying to kill you? No sudden burst of magic?" Minerva asked, her eyes narrowing.

"Nothing," I said. "I was about to be impaled on the end of a tacky ceremonial knife when Jesse hit Grant with a saucepan. The only magical thing around here is that tiny violin…" I pointed to where it had been, but it had disappeared.

"Illusion magic is one of the first natural magics young witches are able to perform. It's simple," Linda said brightly.

Minerva noticed the disappointment on my face. "Every witch must find her path. We all had to start somewhere. We will be here to guide you as your mentors. That's why we came back to Wormwood."

"Thanks… Aunties," I said, saying it out loud for the first time. If it weren't for them coming into town, and me going looking for rental properties, I never would have figured out Grant Kingsley's masterplan. I decided I wouldn't be sharing that little detail. I'd been feeling less than welcoming to family who hadn't acknowledged my existence, until I was suddenly all 'interesting' to them. Things were different now. I understood that they were here for me. What's more, it was actually nice to not have to live alone with only cats for company. Especially when one of those cats was Hemlock.

But as much as I loved having them to stay… there were a few things we needed to talk about. It felt like the right time, now that I knew one of my aunts was loaded.

"I've been keeping this from you because you're my guests and you're family... but I'm kind of broke," I confessed. Tonight was becoming a night for getting all secrets out in the open.

"We know," Linda said.

"Your mother, Freya, was never what you might call a savvy businesswoman. She used to give away too much and spend the rest of her time on petty disputes with people she'd picked fights with," my more serious aunt explained.

Having grown up with my mother, I wasn't going to argue with any of that. "I just want to do what she wanted and keep the shop open, but it's tough. I had a couple of good days this week, when people came in for the old spell bags and you really helped me out by making more... but it's not enough," I explained. "I'm hoping that one day the magazine will pull its weight, but it's only been going for five issues. The next one will be the sixth. I don't yet have enough advertisers to do much more than cover my costs and buy a week's worth of food shopping. Not that I'm complaining. It's just... not as easy as I thought it would be," I surmised.

"Nothing ever is," Minerva said wisely.

"That's not true at all. There's a spell for... Mmmmph!" Linda said, silenced by something Minerva did with a wave of her hand. I squinted and was able to pick out a trail of dark blue. It looked like a magical rag had been stuffed in her sister's mouth.

I blinked and the image was gone.

"Cheats never prosper. Your Aunt Linda is an excellent example of what not to do. You can ask her about it when she can talk again."

"Mmmmph!" Linda complained, folding her arms and glaring daggers Minerva's way.

"In the meantime, I'm sure I speak for both of us when I say we are happy to help out - whether it's by running the shop or paying your bills. This is your home now and your business. We're your aunts, and it's our job to look after you." She smiled a warm smile. All of a sudden, there was a lump in my throat.

"Thank you. It's nice to have a family," I said, pulling them both in for a hug. I blinked. Dark blue, magenta, and gold interwove with each other, creating a beautiful kaleidoscope of colour and light.

It's getting easier, I thought and felt a wild thrill rush through me.

This is magic!

SECRETS AND SHADOWS

The police visited the next morning to tie up a few loose ends. In spite of Detective Admiral's warning, Grant Kingsley wasn't pressing charges against me. He was far too busy employing lawyers to defend him against the allegations I was making and those brought against him by his murderous pawns, Daniel and Jasmine. The detective took the opportunity to remind me that these lawyers may yet change their mind on whether or not to bring up my breaking and entering, but that had been the worst of it. A few questions later and they were gone. Detective Admiral had been the first one to leave. He hadn't looked back.

In the end, I managed to write up the lead article for the local magazine, including all of the arrested suspects and the inside story (minus a few of the details - I was not stupid enough to admit any lawbreaking in print). The magazine was due out next week when February began, and I had a feeling it was going to be the most popular issue yet.

Wormwood was a nosy town. People knew that Grant Kingsley had been arrested for trying to kill someone, and they knew that *someone* was me. Even though several residents had popped into the shop and tried to ask prying questions, I'd kept my silence. I had a free magazine to sell advertising space in, and this was how I was going to do it.

Three days after everything had happened, Tristan Coltrain popped into the shop with a basket full of cakes and pastries.

"Hey, Hazel. How are you holding up?" He walked over to the counter and gave me a hug. "I brought you some things in case you were still in shock."

I looked up from the cupcake I'd already launched into.

Tristan laughed. "Okay... definitely not in shock."

"Are we still in a fake relationship?" I asked, chomping my way through a cupcake that tasted vaguely like Turkish Delight.

"Do I need an excuse like a fake relationship to bring you a basket of the good stuff?"

I raised my eyebrows at him.

Tristan crossed his arms. "Obviously, the answer to that question is 'no'. Although - if those cupcakes do what they say on the tin, you might decide you want me to be your sugar-muffin for real."

I choked on the icing. "What did you just say?!"

Tristan laughed. "They're something I'm trying out before Valentine's Day. They're cupcakes of love... give one to the girl you like, and she'll fall head over heels for you."

"What am I? Your guinea pig?" I complained. When Tristan looked away out of the shop window for a moment, I squinted at the cake. Nothing glowed. It would appear that The Bread Cauldron Bakery genuinely did run on good baking and gimmicks.

"You know... you were asking me for business tips a while back. The first thing I would do is to have seasonal window displays. You've had the nightmare *Children of Corn* picnic thing going on since I got here."

"I've been meaning to change that for ages. I guess I'll have time to do it now that my aunts are helping out around the shop." Aunt Linda and Aunt Minerva were working on stock lists as we spoke.

"I'm sure it will make a difference. Not that you need it. I've been hearing all kinds of people saying all kinds of good things about this place recently. Are you doing something differently?"

"Oh, you know... this and that," I said, thinking of the magical aura around me that was growing by the day, Wormwood residents in the know now treated me with fear and respect in equal measures. It was an interesting change of affairs.

"Is Aurelia still bothering you?" I asked. Tristan must have taken the advice I'd given him to not accept anything to eat or drink from her and to check his pockets regularly. Otherwise, he'd probably be drooling over her right this second.

"I think she's gone off me. Ever since that new guy came into town, my proposition numbers have taken a nosedive. I guess I'm not the new kid in town anymore." He shrugged and pretended to look tragic.

"Are they still buying your cakes?"

"They're all brokenhearted because this guy doesn't even notice they exist, so... yes. More now than ever before."

I grinned. "Sounds like you don't need a fake girlfriend."

"Are you fake breaking up with me?"

We smiled at each other. I felt a rush of warm fuzzy feelings for Tristan. There was nothing magical about him at all, but somehow, I liked him all the better for it.

"I don't mind keeping things casual... in case the stranger leaves town again. Plus, I want my business lessons... and cakes," I added, taking another bite of the love cupcake, having decided it did nothing more than taste excellent.

"In that case, how can I refuse? You've charmed me off my feet." Tristan pretended to swoon on top of the potted plants.

"Don't you start on them! I have enough trouble with the cats."

My friend grinned and gently patted a ginger plant. "I'll call round soon for those business talks. See you, fake girlfriend!"

"Goodbye, fake boyfriend," I said back to him, still smiling even as he walked out the door.

I had just returned to doing the month's bookkeeping, whilst I waited for customers to come in, when Aunt Linda poked her head around the door of the stock room. "Urgh, it's like I can see the love hearts from over here. Will you two just get together already?"

"We're friends!" I protested. "I am not ruining a perfectly good friendship."

"So, you do like him!" Aunt Linda sounded victorious.

"I didn't say that. Some things shouldn't change."

Aunt Linda rolled her eyes. "Spoken like a true Wormwooder."

I grinned. I didn't mind being called that any more. I was no longer running away from the place I had come from. This was where I belonged - in the stagnant puddle of Wormwood, where nothing ever seemed to change.

The evening was mild when I stepped out of the shop at the end of the day. Although it was still January, I thought I could smell the promise of spring, drifting in on a west wind. Everything on my 'to do' list had been ticked off. I was rewarding myself with a walk.

I hadn't expected my feet to carry me into Wormwood Forest. The sun was all but gone, so only shadows greeted me when I walked beneath the trees. I knew the stars would come out soon, but for now, I walked in darkness, feeling the forest around me.

I was not afraid.

The last time I had walked through here, I'd feared that every shadow was a killer waiting to strike, but a lot had changed in the time that had passed since my last trip into the woods. I was learning why a witch has little to fear from the darkness. And the world is never a truly dark place. Not when you have witch sight.

I used it now and was amazed to see a trail of glowing green sigils, illuminating a path through the trees that I sensed had been used by Wormwood's magical community for many years. I had no doubt that this path led into the heart of the forest, to the site where Zack Baden had met his end. I wondered if anyone went there anymore. Would Wormwood forget, or was the site forever desecrated? There was only one way to find out.

I hesitated on the edge of the clearing, the same way I had the first time. I was better at using witch sight now and could maintain it for long periods. When I looked around, I was finally treated to the reason why this clearing was so special to all the magic workers in town.

It was a rainbow formed of all the colours of magic. Pink, blue, red, orange, purple, green, yellow, silver... there were streaks of magic everywhere, indicating that many spells had been cast here, and many protections had been put in place.

But there was something else, too. I noticed places where it looked as though the magic had been eaten away by a dark stain of nothingness. It focused around where the body would have been, at the heart of the summoning sigil. I remembered that the sigil had been a genuine one, whilst the paint on the trees had been mere horror film fluff. I knelt down by the dead space and slowly reached out a hand to touch it. It didn't feel that different, just sort of... empty. I watched as the threads of magic that surrounded me mingled with the space and disappeared.

Oh.

It was like a magical void.

I concentrated and the aura of magic around me disappeared completely.

"Impressive. You're a quick learner."

I stood up and turned around to face Jesse Heathen. "Have you been following me?"

"No. I have my own business in the forest tonight, but it's hard to miss a bright gold magical ball walking through the trees."

"Ball?!" I had not eaten that many cakes! Having said that, Tristan's gift basket was looking rather depleted...

Jesse grinned. "Don't be so touchy," he said, adding that magical smoothness to his voice that charmed everyone. I saw it leave him as a thread of golden light. I wafted it away with a hand.

The expression on Jesse's face was priceless.

"I knew you were cheating!" I told him. "No one has that much charisma naturally."

Jesse recovered and gave me his usual slanting smile. "Ah well, I've still got my looks. You really saw that?" He looked curious.

"It was magic, wasn't it?"

He nodded, but I didn't think he was telling me everything. *No surprise there...*

A slim black shape slunk into the clearing and leaned against Jesse's leg.

We both looked down at Hedge.

"He's your cat, isn't he? We had a good chat on the way in," Jesse casually announced.

"You… chatted?"

"In a manner of speaking."

I pursed my lips, again feeling like he was hiding something - or in Jesse's case, hiding everything. I shot Hedge a disapproving look. He was fraternising with the enemy.

"Will this clearing ever recover?" I asked.

"Probably, in time, or with some concerted effort. You've seen the voids. They happen when energy has been consumed and continues to be taken. In this case, a man died inside a summoning circle, which triggered the energy exchange."

"The circle worked? Isn't that… really bad?" There was still so much I didn't know about magic and its consequences.

"It worked in that it took the energy it was given, but that's it. It takes more than that to open up a portal to some dark place."

"Some dark place? Is that what we're calling it?"

"It's not as simple as you think."

"It might be if you explained," I muttered, ready to turn around and walk out on this conversation.

We stood in silence for a few moments with neither one of us willing to back down.

"I suppose you'll be leaving town now that the murder is solved?" I said, determined to at least score a few points with the amount of disdain I managed to ladle over those words.

"I'm sticking around for a while. There are a few things I still need to do." Jesse pushed his hands deep into the pockets of his black jeans and looked cool and mysterious.

Urgh. He was the worst.

I shook my head and turned to leave the clearing. Hedge

would have to make his own decision, but I was definitely going to be having words with him about his questionable taste in people... and giant black hounds with glowing red eyes.

"Hazel..." Jesse said.

I turned and looked back at him, giving him one last chance to say something worthwhile. If this whole drama had taught me anything, it was that you should only be friends with people you were sure of - people you could trust. Jesse Heathen was not falling into that category right now.

"This is just one of the first symptoms of the changes that are coming. I think you know it, too." He narrowed his eyes and watched me.

I considered. Was Wormwood finally changing, and not for the better? "I'm not sure," I said, honestly.

Jesse looked at me seriously with his amber eyes. "Mark my words. Things are going to change around here, and you're involved."

"Me? Why? You have to tell me more than that!" This was the most frustrating conversation ever.

Jesse's smile was infuriating. "I can't. I shouldn't even be saying this much. Just know that I am on your side."

I threw my hands up in the air. "Great! That clears everything up." I regarded him across the clearing.

Then, I asked the question I felt sure would unlock all of the other answers, if he would only tell the truth. "Who are you?"

Jesse's sideways smile was immediate. I knew it for what it was - a sign that he was going to dodge this question, like all the others I'd asked. "You're not ready to believe it yet."

Then he was gone, disappearing into the shadows for the second time.

I stood alone in the clearing with Hedge. "Do you want to

come home, or do you have a busy schedule full of meetings with questionable characters?" I asked him.

"Meow," Hedge said, just as I was turning away.

My head snapped back round, but the black cat was silent again. "Please tell me that wasn't my imagination?" I said to the silent cat.

He blinked once and then trotted out of the clearing, leading the way back home.

I stood there for a moment longer, wondering if he really had made his second ever meow… and if I really had seen the blue glow of magic leaving his mouth when he'd done it.

It seemed like everyone in Wormwood had a secret to hide, even my pet cat.

A REVIEW IS WORTH ITS WEIGHT IN GOLD!

I really hope you enjoyed reading this story. I was wondering if you could spare a couple of moments to rate and review this book? As an indie author, one of the best ways you can help support my dream of being an author is to leave me a review on your favourite online book store, or even tell your friends.

Reviews help other readers, just like you, to take a chance on a new writer!

Thank you!
Ruby Loren

ALSO BY RUBY LOREN

MADIGAN AMOS ZOO MYSTERIES

Penguins and Mortal Peril

The Silence of the Snakes

Murder is a Monkey's Game

Lions and the Living Dead

The Peacock's Poison

A Memory for Murder

Whales and a Watery Grave

Chameleons and a Corpse

Foxes and Fatal Attraction

Monday's Murderer

Prequel: Parrots and Payback

DIANA FLOWERS FLORICULTURE MYSTERIES

Gardenias and a Grave Mistake

Delphiniums and Deception

Poinsettias and the Perfect Crime

Peonies and Poison

The Lord Beneath the Lupins

Prequel: The Florist and the Funeral

HOLLY WINTER MYSTERIES

Snowed in with Death

A Fatal Frost

Murder Beneath the Mistletoe

Winter's Last Victim

EMILY HAVERSSON OLD HOUSE MYSTERIES

The Lavender of Larch Hall

The Leaves of Llewellyn Keep

The Snow of Severly Castle

The Frost of Friston Manor

The Heart of Heathley House

HAYLEY ARGENT HORSE MYSTERIES

The Swallow's Storm

The Starling's Summer

The Falcon's Frost

The Waxwing's Winter

JANUARY CHEVALIER SUPERNATURAL MYSTERIES

Death's Dark Horse

Death's Hexed Hobnobs

Death's Endless Enchanter

Death's Ethereal Enemy

Death's Last Laugh

Prequel: Death's Reckless Reaper

BLOOMING SERIES

Blooming

Abscission

Frost-Bitten

Blossoming

Flowering

Fruition

Made in the USA
Middletown, DE
23 May 2019